JUSTICE

He rode into Buffalo, sun-darkened, dusty—and smelling of danger—a big man with a Winchester in his saddle boot and a gunbelt that looked like an old friend.

His name was Roderick, Sergeant Will Roderick out of Fort Abraham Lincoln. The town had lynched his younger brother only days before.

Roderick was there to find out who and why—in a town of casual justice and whisky-fast draws—a town that waited for him to make his move . . . and didn't realize it was out of its class in fighting a man who had spent a lifetime in the business of fighting the Indians.

SADDLE JUSTICE

Steven C. Lawrence

GUNSMOKE

This hardback edition 2008
by BBC Audiobooks Ltd
by arrangement with
Golden West Literary Agency

ISBN 978 1 405 68213 8

British Library Cataloguing in Publication Data available.

Printed and bound in Great Britain by
CPI Antony Rowe, Chippenham, Wiltshire

1

ONE Tuesday afternoon in July, just after four, a dusty rider broke from the willow thicket lining the Platte north of Buffalo. Two Mexican women filling deep wooden buckets at one of the river's backwater pools glanced around to view the man who had pulled up his big horse abruptly and now sat as if musing, studying the town.

Will Roderick paid no attention to the women. A slight pressure from his knees moved the black gelding forward four long-striding steps to a spot well clear of the watchers. Then the animal again turned motionless as a statue. The Mexican women frowned knowingly and returned to their chore. They kept their backs held stiff and faces lowered, as though they had in some way done wrong to turn and stare at the rider.

Actually, Roderick had moved simply to get clear of the great cloud of mosquitoes humming along the gleaming white sandbars that thrust outward into the sluggish, gurgling current. He had been riding for longer than four days, working deeper and deeper into Nebraska Territory, and now that he was at his destination he could feel his tenseness coming back.

He had expected that, though.

While he considered the feeling, he took papers and a tobacco sack from the pocket of his sweat-stained gray shirt. He spun a cigarette into shape. After lighting it he smoked calmly, but his appraising glances were alert, and there was a steady cold spark in his dark eyes.

Roderick was a long man close to thirty, big of bone, with a firm maturity in his weather-darkened face. He wore a gunbelt and faded denim trousers that were held into tight cylinder shapes where they were drawn over high-heeled boots. The stock of a Winchester rifle pro-

5

truded from a new, shining leather boot beneath his right
knee. Since he'd left the Fort Abraham Lincoln garrison,
he'd spent lots of time picturing Buffalo, and he was close
to being right about it at that.

A dusty, sun-beaten town, one of a string spotting the
snaking length of the Union Pacific, a town made by and
kept alive by the railroad. During the early seventies, before Roderick had gone back into the army, he'd been on
drives to Ogallala and other railheads like Buffalo. He had
known that he could expect anything in those bustling,
wild towns. Now, in seventy-five, though there were still
a few towns like Abilene and Ellsworth and Dodge, you
should expect less wildness in these smaller railheads. From
cowhands who had made the latest long drive, he had
heard how it was getting to be tamer, quieter, and with
more and stricter law all along the trail.

That was what he'd heard. But it wasn't true here, he
knew. The intense quiet of Buffalo was as misleading as the
false fronts that lined its main street. Because of this
knowledge, Roderick's hard eyes were cautious and his
big body remained slightly hunched as he swung the black
to the left and onto the dirt road running parallel to the
railroad. Entering the town like any visitor, he could study
everything along Center Street, and also judge the handiest
ways of leaving, if he had to in a hurry.

Once past the ramshackle, crowded shanties of the Mexican section workers at the edge of the flat, he slowed his
mount to a walk. On the right there was a corral, and directly opposite stood a block of small sheds used for storage,
and the livery barn. Beyond that, on both sides, a sprinkling
of small homes with little fenced lawns and flower beds
under the cottonwoods and greyish, green tamarisks were
lined neatly along the cross streets.

In the business district, Will Roderick's attention was
drawn by the many signs reading "No Mex" and "Mexicans Not Wanted" on doors and fences and walls. As he
crossed an intersection, a barefooted Mexican boy stepped
down from the boardwalk. The youth halted in the heated
dust to let the horse pass. He kept his eyes downward, as
if studying the black's hoofs.

Roderick stopped. The boy turned to go back onto the
walk.

"Hey," said Roderick in Spanish, "do you know where
a lawyer named Porter has his office?"

The boy was about thirteen, wearing torn and filthy cheap cotton pants. A blank, frightened expression had come onto his face. He eyed the rider.

"Well, do you know?" Broderick repeated.

"You mean the judge, señor?" Nervously, the boy rubbed one grimy hand across his mouth. "Judge is only lawyer I know of." He gestured towards the line of fine white houses with big half-glass doors at the east end of town. "He lives down there."

Nodding, Roderick said, "Where's his office?"

"Over in the courthouse. He . . ." His voice fell off as a thin, gray-haired man coming along the boardwalk stepped down to cross the street. The boy's eyes dropped to his knobby bare feet and the dust.

Roderick glanced at the man, and he saw that there was much resentment behind the heavy beard. He felt as much confused by the clear hostility in the man's face as by the boy's hopelessness.

With a frown Roderick turned back to the boy. "You go over to the judge's office and see if he's in there." He dug into his pocket and drew out a coin. "I'll be up at the hotel."

The boy did not take the money. "I cannot go into the hotel, señor. There has been trouble." He shook his head. "I cannot take your money, señor."

"Well, you can have a look, anyway." Roderick leaned over and put the coin into the boy's hand. "Wait in front of the hotel till I come out."

"But one of my people murdered a man. I want no trouble, señor."

At that, Roderick's face tightened. "A Mexican was in on the murder?" he asked.

"Yes. He and a gringo shot a man."

"What was the gringo's name?"

"Roderick." The boy spat the words. "Chico Roderick."

Will Roderick's eyes hardened. "You get over and see if Porter's in his office." His voice was quick, tight. "Go ahead. Vamoose!"

He straightened in his saddle and pulled the black to the left, then rode past the general store, two saloons facing each other across the width of the street, a restaurant, and beyond that a block that had recently been completely burned. He stopped before the Shiloh Hotel and, dismounting, whipped a halter knot around the worn hitchrail.

While he unloaded his blanket roll, he glanced back along Center.

The bearded man who'd been so antagonistic now stood in front of the bank. He was staring toward the hotel. There was no doubt about him; his gaze, directed at Roderick, was questioning and insolent.

Roderick wondered about that. Maybe he'd had a part in it. Maybe? There had been a time in Will Roderick's life when he would have gone back and asked some questions. Now he dismissed that thought as rash, useless. His business here might later include the bearded man, but he'd have to know all the facts before showing any belligerence.

For a moment he stared back. Then he took his sombrero off and beat the dust from his clothing and roll. He drew his Winchester, secured it under his arm, and went up onto the hotel's porch.

Inside, he moved slowly until his eyes became accustomed to the dark. A stale odor of fried bacon and eggs lingered in the comparatively cool air of the lobby. Placed neatly about the carpetless floor were a battered leather divan and three cane-backed chairs, each guarding a polished brass spittoon. A flickering coal-oil lamp hanging above the desk threw shadows across the key rack and ancient lithographs on the walls.

Roderick stopped at the desk and leaned the roll and rifle against the counter. Somewhere above him a door closed. He took off his sombrero and wiped his forehead as he looked beyond the desk to a narrow staircase rising to the top floor. After another minute, he lifted the Winchester and put it down again, this time letting it bang the desk hollowly.

The staircase creaked, and a short, fat man whose balding head and round face gave an impression of geniality came down. He wore a clean white shirt, sleeves rolled up. A thick silver watch chain swung from a pocket in his vest.

"Howdy," the clerk said pleasantly. He crowded in behind the desk. "Single room?"

Nodding, Roderick told him, "I should be here a week. Maybe two."

"Number seven . . ." the clerk began, but he paused before opening the registration ledger. For a moment he gazed at the tall man opposite him, his eyes resting on the flat planes of the dark-burned face and black hair parted deep on the side. Shortly, as though he had made up his mind about something, he laid the ledger open on the counter.

"Sign here," he said, taking a pencil from his vest pocket. "Dollar-fifty a day."

Silently, the clerk waited while Roderick wrote, the quiet broken only by the scratch of the lead. When Roderick finished, the clerk took a key from the rack.

"Toilet's at the end of the hall. Spittoon's changed each mornin'." He held out the key.

Roderick took it. He bent and lifted his roll and rifle and went along the darkened corridor.

The moon-faced clerk swung the ledger around. His jowls tightened as he studied the name. William Roderick. Fort Abraham Lincoln. He glanced up then, as the door opened, letting in the sharp glare of sunlight. The gray-bearded man had entered and was coming up to the desk.

The clerk closed the ledger and started for the stairs.

"Say, Bainbridge," the bearded man called, "you got a minute?"

Bainbridge glanced around. "What is it now, Harry?" he said, his voice annoyed. "Lose your key again?"

Harry Stewart looked down at the ledger. "That rider that just come in?" He waited, expecting an answer.

"He took Number Seven."

For a moment silence lay hard between them. Stewart's eyes came up, and he nodded toward the corridor. "What's his name? He was mighty friendly with a greaser kid."

"So?"

"He could be a Mex, you know."

The fat clerk smiled slightly, but there was no mirth in it. "Hell, Harry, you got Mexes on the brain. He wasn't no Mex."

"You ask him?"

"Didn't have to ask." Bainbridge shook his head sadly. "You're carryin' this thing too far, Harry. The Mexicans here are good people. You can't . . ."

"Look . . . I ain't forgittin' Mike Haven was a good friend of mine."

"Mike was my friend, too, Harry," said Bainbridge. "But Chico's dead, and they'll get Lerraza. You got no right to keep after every other Mex in town."

Stewart fingered the brush of his beard. "You say that, when you know they had trouble on the section last week? You shoulda kept your sign up like everyone else."

"Harry, that rider wasn't a Mex. He . . ." Bainbridge hesitated, then shrugged his fat shoulders. "His name's Roderick." He kept his voice casual, but watched for Stewart's reaction.

But the bearded face didn't change at all. "Well, sure. You know the judge said there was a will," he answered. And, as if explaining, "I just didn't want no Mex comin' here to cause trouble."

"No reason why there should be trouble, Harry." Bainbridge paused, and then added, "Should there be, Harry?"

Stewart stared at him. "Meanin'?"

"Meanin' that stranger ain't no Mex, so he's got a right to be here, ain't he?"

Down the darkened corridor there was the sound of a door opening. Stewart, fingering his beard, glanced that way. He managed to nod, but his resentment was still there.

Will Roderick closed and locked the door before walking toward the lobby. He had waited in the small, hot room until he judged the Mexican boy had had ample time to get to the hotel. Now he noticed Stewart was standing by the desk. He was looking his way, his bearded face furtively indifferent.

There's too much worry there, Roderick felt. He hadn't figured on trouble coming right away, for he had thought he'd have to do the pushing. But this man could force things. He didn't want that. He'd need time to look around, time to think it all out, time to decide just what he should do.

Annoyed, he stared at Stewart, who looked away warily. Roderick nodded to the fat clerk. He walked through the lobby, opened the door, and went across the porch and down to the boardwalk.

The Mexican youth was waiting in the street. When Roderick stepped off the walk, the boy gestured toward the east.

"Judge Porter went home, señor," he said. "Left the courthouse three minutes now."

Roderick glanced at the line of big, fine homes. "Which house is his?"

"Last on the right, señor, with the big barn behind." The boy turned to leave.

"Wait." Roderick pointed to the hitchrail. "Take my horse over to the livery and tell the hostler to . . ."

"I can't go into the barn." The boy bit his lower lip, his black eyes flickering beyond Roderick to the porch.

Roderick turned and saw Stewart standing there.

"Gracias, kid," he said, feeling his irritation growing to anger. He stared directly into the bearded face, his eyes hard.

Stewart's cheeks flushed; then, looking away from the stare, he came down the steps and went along the walk.

"You go ahead now, kid," Roderick said. The youth ran down the street, his bare feet kicking up small bursts of dust.

Roderick gave a friendly slap on the gelding's neck. He untied the black and, taking the bridle, led him past the line of stores and through the work area in front of the livery barn.

He halted at a wooden water trough to let the animal drink.

From inside came a cough, and then a man smoking a brier pipe appeared from out of the shadows between the two rows of stalls. The hostler, tall, with a long face, stopped in the open doorway and watched Roderick. He was a businessman who wasn't partial to strangers these days, and there was nothing discreet about his stare.

"Come far?" he asked.

"Dakota," Roderick said. "You want to water him easy and give him a good rub?"

"If you're a Mex, I can't do nothin' for you. We've had trouble here." He pulled the door half closed and motioned with his thumb at the sign tacked there reading "No Mex."

Roderick eyed the sign, then held the bridle out to the hostler. "Put him in one of those back stalls, so he don't get the sun," he said.

"I had to ask, mister. I just work here. Don't want no trouble." He took the bridle and nodded at the black. "Army mount, I'd say."

"You know your horses," Roderick said. For another minute he watched the animal drink. Finally he turned and walked from the work area.

As he went along Center Street, Roderick kept an eye

out for the bearded man, but he saw no sign that he was
still being watched. Some cowhands rode past, none showing interest in him. Three women stood talking in front
of the milliner's shop, their conversation holding all their
attention. Not one of the boys playing kick-the-can looked
his way as he crossed the street. And, when he went by
the Silver Dollar Saloon, one of the two men just coming
out edged behind the other to allow him room to pass.

Roderick let himself relax. Actually, it didn't matter
to most people that he was a stranger. Because a Mexican
had been in on the killing, it was natural for a few like
the bearded man to keep the race feeling alive. His coming
here like this would get him some of that, too, he knew.
If trouble came he wouldn't run from it, but neither did
he intend to provoke the diehards. He'd just have to be
extra careful of them.

Harry Stewart walked hurriedly through the crowded bar
of the Silver Dollar to where a man was sitting alone at
one of the back tables. The man was younger than Stewart,
leanly muscular, with a thin mouth and bland, cunning
eyes, not the eyes that went with the working cowhand's
clothing he wore.

Stewart muttered quick words to the seated man.

"You're sure he's alone, Harry?"

Nodding, Stewart answered, "Bainbridge knew it was
Roderick, and he still let him a room. Somethin' oughtta
be done about that, Curly."

"He's headed for the judge's?"

"Yeah . . . Curly, you oughtta take care of this right
away. Finish him off quick."

Curly Gromm shook his head. "Moe gets first crack,"
he said.

"But Roderick's carryin' a gun."

"We'll do it like Mr. Wayne said," Curly told him.
"Moe was Haven's best friend. It'll just be a grudge fight.
This way the ranch ain't in it at all."

He stood, walked to the half-frosted window and looked
out. In front of the hotel the building's shadow was long
and wide in the lowering sun. Heat's shimmering dazzle
flashed from metal on a homesteader's buggy tied to a
hitchrail there. The same sun reflected in a white glare
from the window of the saloon, but Curly could make out
a man just turning into Judge Porter's walk.

Without speaking, Curly pushed his way through the batwings and strode across Center towards the blacksmith's shop. His two guns were thonged low and tight to his thighs, so the length of his fingers brushed their bone handles. Following him, Stewart hung back a little, letting Curly go into Moe Duff's first.

Duff, a huge man with tremendous arms and shoulders, glanced up from the shoe he was pounding into shape.

Curly Gromm said, "Roderick's here, Moe. Just went up to the judge's."

The blacksmith stared absently at the red-hot shoe, then took a few final blows at it. When he looked up again there was a frown on his wide face.

"Wayne says two hundred this time," he said pointedly.

"Two hundred," Curly repeated, "for a good job."

"I don't know," Stewart offered. "Maybe you should handle this yourself, Curly. Roderick'll be . . ."

Duff cursed. "You think I can't handle him?" His immense jaws tightened as his look shifted to Stewart.

"Hell no, Moe. But you don't carry a gun. I just thought that . . ."

"Then shut up. You talk too much."

Harry Stewart frowned. He drew back a step as Duff turned away from the anvil. He hadn't missed the implication of the blacksmith's sharp words, and he knew the threat there. He'd seen Moe beat more than one man senseless with his powerful fists. In a way he was glad he'd angered the big man. Roderick wouldn't stand a chance with Duff riled like this.

Duff lifted one hairy arm and wiped the sweat from his forehead. "Some broken bones?" he said to Curly.

"Anythin' you want. Mr. Wayne says this one's wide open. The town'll be with you when they see who he is."

The blacksmith smiled and started for the door.

"Don't go up there," Curly said. "Wait 'til he's clear of the judge's."

The smile vanished. Duff shot back a look of patient contempt. "My job," he said. "I handle it my way. You just have my two hundred ready."

When Duff was outside, Stewart stepped cautiously forward. He stared at Curly in amazement.

"You let him talk to you like that?" he asked.

Curly nodded carelessly. "The boss said to let Moe have first crack," he replied. "That's all I'm doin', Harry."

2

ON JUDGE PORTER'S porch Will Roderick cranked the large doorbell and waited. Shortly, soft footsteps sounded inside the house. He took one last glance along the street, but he still couldn't see anyone watching him. When the door was opened he turned his head back again.

A pretty blonde girl of about nineteen stood there. She wore no make-up and was dressed in a full brown skirt and white blouse buttoned primly to the throat. Her large gray eyes surveyed Roderick timidly.

"Yes?" she said.

"I'd like to see Judge Porter. I have a letter from him."

Directly behind the girl an older woman's voice called, "Who is it, Lucy?" And then a thin, sharp-nosed woman who carried her head high came into the hallway. Her black dress rustled gently as she moved. "Yes, young man," she asked stiffly, "what can I do for you?"

"He wants to see the judge, Auntie," the girl began. "He has a . . ."

"Go back to your lunch, dear." The woman stepped into the doorway, edging the girl behind her. "Tell Judge Porter he has a visitor."

Before leaving, the girl offered Roderick a quick, apologetic smile, but he looked away toward the other woman.

"Warm day," he said.

The woman nodded slowly. Her gaze had covered his dusty, sweat-streaked clothing, and now she stood with her neck and back held stiff.

"My husband will be here soon." She made no move to let him in.

Quick footsteps sounded in the hall, and a heavy-set, white-haired man in his late fifties walked to the doorway. "You wished to see me?" he asked in a deep voice. There was an air of amiable pomposity about him.

"My name's Roderick. You sent me a letter, Judge."

"Sergeant Roderick . . . of course." Judge Porter's wide face broke into a smile. "Come inside, Sergeant. We can talk in my den."

He stepped back to let Roderick enter. At the same time he looked at his wife. She wore a listening expression, as if she had heard something she found disagreeable.

"I'll take care of the sergeant, Alma," the judge said, and he led the way from the hall. Roderick followed him through a spotlessly clean dark parlor furnished with large horsehair chairs and a sofa.

Judge Porter opened a door at the end of the room and stood aside to let Roderick enter first. The den was small, its ceiling-high shelves lined with handsomely bound legal volumes. The judge went behind his long mahogany desk.

He said conversationally, "You reached here sooner than I expected, with conditions on the frontier as bad as they are."

"I got in from patrol the morning the mail came, Judge."

Roderick sat down in an overstuffed leather chair.

"And you're certain our Roderick was your brother."

"That picture you sent was Charlie, Judge."

Roderick took a bulky, soiled envelope from a rear pocket and pushed it across the desk. "You can check with Major Reno at the fort about these papers." He added, troubled, "I heard there was a Mexican in on the killing."

"Yes. Pablo Lerraza. He worked for Chico. But the mob didn't get him."

A thinking hardness lurked around Roderick's eyes. Chico . . . he recalled the "No Mex" signs and how the boy had spat out that name. "Just how did Charlie tie in with the Mexicans?" he asked.

"He was a big man with them, Sergeant. He owned the cantina and hotel they used. And he was their representative in the town council." Judge Porter hesitated, rubbed his smooth chin and asked, "Was there any Mexican blood in your family?"

"No."

The judge was silent for a moment. Then he said quietly, "People connected your brother to the Mexicans. Some here still believe he was part Mexican. Since the killing it's been very hard for those people."

Roderick considered that, thinking of the bearded man. He asked finally, "You think maybe those lynchers didn't like the idea of Charlie being so close to the Mexicans?"

The judge shook his head. "I told you about the murder in my letter, Sergeant."

"But there was no trial?"

"No. With Sheriff Nye out of town on business, there was no one to hold the mob down. Haven's friends lynched Chico as soon as they caught him." He opened the top desk drawer and took out some papers. "This is the recorded testimony of the inquest. Two cowhands from Running W saw Chico and Lerraza ride off from Haven's body. And Maria Jack heard Chico arguing with Haven that morning in the cantina."

"Then I reckon the people I got to see are those cowhands. And this Maria."

Judge Porter held out the papers, but Roderick did not take them.

Roderick said evenly, "I'd rather talk to those witnesses first. I'll read that later."

"Sergeant, if you go looking for trouble, it'll only make it harder on the Mexicans here. Things have quieted down this last week. There are no posses out looking for Lerraza now. They figure he's probably in Mexico anyway. But, if you start forcing things, it'll wake the whole feeling again."

"My kid brother was lynched, Judge."

Nodding, the white-haired man spoke plainly, all sign of pomposity gone now. "The two men who led the lynch mob are in the county jail. We had a quick trial, and they got three years. And the sheriff fired the deputy who let them lynch Chico." He added, "It's straightened out the best we could. You can only make it worse all around."

Roderick stood. "How long'll it be till you get the will cleared up?"

"By the weekend. I've had a good offer for the block that was burned. There'll be some money from that also."

"The same mob burned Charlie's buildings, too?"

"That was done right after the lynching. You've got to realize what it was like, Sergeant. There was a great deal of hate here those first few days."

Roderick thought about that. "Well, I'd like to talk to those witnesses, Judge. Asking them what happened shouldn't cause any trouble."

"Very well, then. I'll send someone out to get Forbes and Thompson."

"No. I'll ride out. Where does Maria live?"

"I don't know where the girl is." The judge stood up slowly. "But if you follow the river north six or seven miles you can't miss the Running W." Coming around the desk, he extended his hand. "Tell Dan Wayne I sent you out."

Roderick took the hand. He asked, "Where's Charlie buried?"

"In the Mexican cemetery. His grave isn't marked, though."

Roderick's voice was tense. "You order a stone," he said. "Take anything you need from the will."

Nodding, Judge Porter was silent. He led the way into the hallway and let Roderick out. When he shut the front door he heard the rustle of his wife's starched dress behind him. He looked around at her and saw her mouth was set in a furious, thin line.

"What do you mean by having that man come to this house?" she snapped.

The judge dodged her eyes. "I'm handling his brother's will, Alma. If we show friendship, he might not make trouble."

Her stare was unyielding. "And what do you think people are going to say when they see you're helping that murderer's brother?"

"I don't care," he said, dragging out the words. "I just don't want any more killing."

Mrs. Porter shook her head, making no effort to comprehend his reasoning. "I don't understand you," she said. "I'd think you'd let the trouble stay in the saloons where it belongs."

"Alma, the sergeant's brother was lynched in this town."

"And it has nothing to do with the decent people of Buffalo."

Judge Porter spoke slowly. "If the so-called decent people of this town had acted as they should have, Alma, there wouldn't be any reason for Roderick to be here at all." Now, for the first time he met her stare. "You know that just as well as I do."

3

To the west the sun had lost its harsh glare of day. Shadows stretched across the dusty width of Center Street. Townspeople hurried along the walks, doing last-minute shopping; in front of the hardware a clerk was busy lowering the striped awning. Mexican section workers came up from the roundhouse in one large group, moving quietly along the edge of the street. They visibly made an effort to keep to themselves as they headed for their own part of town.

Roderick, walking toward the livery barn, noticed these signs of the finish of a working day, just as he noticed the expression on every face he passed. People treated him as they would any stranger, allowing him only casual glances.

There was no reason for him to doubt the judge's frank statement about the trouble being settled in the best way possible. If the bearded man's brand of anger was all he struck, he'd have little cause to worry. Watchful hostility couldn't keep him from getting every last fact about the lynching.

Looking for the Mexican girl right now would waste time, he felt. He'd talk to the two cowhands first, then find the girl. He was thinking about this when he became aware that a big man whose apelike body bulged out of his work clothing had stepped down from the shadowed porch of the Silver Dollar and was heading toward him.

From his clothing Roderick judged he was a blacksmith. He was not wearing a gun. Something in the way he walked warned Roderick, and he angled his steps to the left, so he wouldn't cross the man's path.

The blacksmith hurried his stride and came to a stop directly in front of Roderick.

"Your name Roderick?" he called in a loud voice. "Your brother the son who killed Mike Haven?"

Roderick's eyes flicked to walks and porches on each side, catching the way people stopped what they'd been doing to watch. Behind him he heard a man's voice say,

"Moe's goin' on another rampage. Somebody get the sheriff."

"Hell, no. You heard him say that's Chico's brother, didn't you?"

A coldness ran up Roderick's spine, and tautness knotted the muscles of his stomach. Right now it was intensely important that the townspeople know the last thing he wanted was any kind of a fight. He held down his anger, started to walk around Moe Duff.

Duff laughed scornfully. "Yellow," he shouted, "just like your brother."

"Look," said Roderick, feeling the sweat on his forehead, "I've got no quarrel with you."

"Mike Haven was my friend, mister."

His name, Roderick decided, didn't matter. It was what he represented, what was behind the beating. Word had been passed around fast, for the piano inside the saloon stopped abruptly and men were spilling out onto the porch. Roderick caught sight of bearded Harry Stewart standing with a cowhand near the bank, but they were suddenly blotted out as the crowd surged from the walks into the street.

"I still have no quarrel with you," Roderick said to Duff. He started on again.

"Git him, Moe," a man yelled. "Git him!"

"Damn right . . ." The blacksmith called an obscene name as he lunged forward, grabbed Roderick's arm and spun him around.

Too late Roderick jerked his arm free and up to ward off the blow he saw coming. Duff's fast, solid smash hit just above the right ear, sending Roderick reeling back.

The two hundred fifty pounds of Duff's body was on him with violent fury, his left connecting with Roderick's stomach, his right pounding into Roderick's face. Pain burst inside Roderick's head as he was slammed down savagely. He heard the tense, excited shouting of the watchers, the deep, frenzied laughter that came from Duff.

Blood flowed from Roderick's torn lip as he pushed himself up. In that instant Duff kicked him mercilessly in the chest. Gasping for breath, Roderick fell flat, twisting wildly to clear the next kick.

Duff's hobnailed boot grazed his forehead. Roderick grabbed at the big foot, got hold, and twisted with all the strength of his body. Duff crashed to the ground.

With amazing swiftness for a man of his bulk, Duff sprang to his feet. His matted black hair and thick-stubbled face had taken on a wild, hateful look.

"All right," he growled. "But don't beg me to quit."

Wet with sweat, Roderick sucked in great breaths as he moved back from the stalking man. He couldn't battle this giant in close. He had to keep clear until he gauged him fully, then make his fight.

Behind him, the bunched men, grinning, refused to part. Roderick began edging to the right. Angry, taunting yells went up. Close by a man shouted, "Get back in there and fight," and someone shoved Roderick forward hard.

Knocked off balance, Roderick stumbled. Duff pounced on him, his body stinking of sweat and smoke. A right made Roderick jackknife, the left that followed hitting high up on the forehead, straightening him.

"You got him now, Moe," a yell came. "Finish him."

Roderick's legs began to give. A roaring filled his head. Duff's thick arm shot out, caught Roderick's shirt front and jerked him forward. Laughing shrilly, Duff circled both arms about Roderick and put on the pressure.

Wildly, Roderick struggled, chopping both fists into the muscular stomach. The squeezing pressure increased steadily. Roderick clawed his fingers into the bristly face, lowering his hand until he got the heel under Duff's chin. He forced the chin up enough to slide his left in beside the right. With tremendous effort, he inched the huge head back, getting leverage, until the left held the chin alone; then he smashed at Duff's face with his right. Duff's nose collapsed, spurting blood.

Duff's grip slackened. His right hand dropped and pawed at Roderick's gunbelt. Roderick jabbed his elbow into the wide chest to push himself clear. The crowd quieted suddenly. Boot heels clattered along the boardwalk, and a horse trotted in the distance. A woman screamed in horror.

A second female voice shouted, "No! No, you'll kill him!"

Duff's right swung into the air. Roderick looked up, saw the silver barrel of his Colt high above his head. One solid blow would make him completely helpless. Total unconsciousness wouldn't stop Duff.

Fear strengthened Roderick. Violently, he pushed himself down and outward, jerking, twisting his body. His outstretched left arm caught the blow, deflecting it from his head.

Again Duff's arm came up, holding the gun poised. Roderick charged in, throwing both hands up to catch the powerful wrist.

They stood with their boots overlapping, the smaller man wrenching at the giant's arm. Roderick suddenly dropped his right, bringing it whacking into the wide-open stomach. Twice more he rammed short, quick blows at the same spot. Duff staggered back.

Roderick gave him no time to regain balance. Lunging at the hand that held the Colt, he gripped the wrist again, and twisted it wildly. His right got hold of the handle, jerked it and wrenched it free.

Duff dove forward. Defensively, Roderick wheeled around, making an arc with the steel barrel. The round-house swing caught Duff solidly across the forehead, ripping a gash between his eyes.

Duff stopped short, dismayed at what had happened. He wiped one hairy arm across his eyes, clearing his vision of the streaming blood.

"I'll kill you . . . kill you," Duff bellowed. He lowered his head and charged.

Roderick threw the Colt behind him as he sidestepped, then brought the flat edges of both hands chopping down onto the bone-hard neck. Knocked off balance by the power of the blow, Duff's arms flayed air and he went sprawling in the dust.

An audible gasp went up from the crowd, followed by silence as Roderick stepped back, allowing the fallen man room to stand. Duff pushed himself onto one knee. The skidding fall had widened the tear in his scalp. Caked blobs of dirt dropped from the wound as blood gushed across his eyes, splashed from his nose and chin.

For a moment there was no sound. The watchers gaped at the half-prostrate giant. Muttering broke out, mumbling about the smaller, lighter man who, breathing deeply, still stood motionless, waiting for the battered blacksmith to get up.

The quiet, hostile faces watched Roderick as he wiped his own bleeding mouth. He saw their looks, wondered how many others who felt the same as Duff would come after him now.

Duff tried to stand. Blinded by his own blood, he reeled

to the left. The crowd surged back, giving him room to regain his balance.

"Hold it, Moe." A stubby, mustached man wearing a tarnished star on his cowhide vest came through the crowd. He was in his early fifties, and there was harsh leanness to his body. "That's enough," he said.

"He was lucky, Jaff," Moe Duff snarled. "I'll kill him!" He spat a mouthful of blood and took a step towards Roderick.

The sheriff blocked his way. "No. You've lost too much blood already."

Duff cursed. His huge frame quivered. He moved forward slowly.

"Here, you men," Sheriff Nye said to some bystanders, "help Moe down to Doc's."

Two cowhands grabbed hold of Duff's arms. The blacksmith tried to wrench himself free, but the men held on. For a few moments Duff stared hazily at Roderick. Finally, he let himself be led through the crowd.

Roderick bent and picked up his Colt. He was checking the barrel to make sure it was clear of dirt, when the sheriff stopped beside him. He stared into Roderick's marked face.

"You come over to my office," Nye said.

"Sheriff, I fought fair."

"I saw that," Nye answered. "I've got your brother's belongings over there. You come and get them."

His eyes moved around at the bystanders. Roderick followed his gaze, seeing how the men were still gathered together along the edge of the walk, looking angry as they watched. It would take only one word, one wrong move for them to turn into a mob.

Sheriff Nye said, "You come along now."

Roderick holstered his Colt and followed the lawman across Center Street.

Once in his office Sheriff Nye left Roderick and went past the iron-rimmed door that led to the cell block. The room, smelling of lamp smoke and Bull Durham tobacco, was small, furnished with a battered rolltop desk and swivel chair, and three cane-backed chairs sitting directly under the gunrack. Roderick crossed the unpainted pine floor and waited near the desk.

Nye reappeared in less than a minute, carrying a dusty

cardboard valise and a rusted Winchester 73 rifle. He came to the desk and, pushing a few papers to one side, laid the valise and carbine down.

"This is all that's left of Chico's stuff," he said.

"Only this, from everything he owned here?"

The lawman nodded. "Most everything went when the cantina was fired."

"Sheriff, you were out of town during the lynching, weren't you?"

"Yes. Checkin' on some beef out at Double A."

"And then you couldn't stop the mob from burning Charlie's building?"

Their stares locked. The veins in Nye's neck seemed to tighten, but he said nothing. Roderick was puzzled. He'd gotten only hate from the crowd. Nye's expression held something different. Not hate, not an absence of hostility, but something more guarded.

In the silence that stretched out an elderly Mexican holding a broom entered from the cell block. He was short-legged and dark as an Indian. He began sweeping the room without looking up.

Roderick tucked the Winchester under his arm, lifted the valise. "Thanks, Sheriff." He started to leave.

The lawman asked, "How long you figure to stay here?"

At that Roderick stopped. "Until I find out everything about the killing."

"Didn't the judge give you the whole story?"

"He told me all he knew. But I figure the witnesses can fill me in better."

He waited. Nye didn't speak. Out of the corner of his eye, Roderick could see that the old Mexican had slowed his sweeping and now watched him with a look of smouldering distrust.

Roderick said slowly, "I want to talk to a girl named Maria Jack, Sheriff. You know where I can find her?"

Nye shook his head. Then, as if a thought had suddenly occurred to him, he looked at the old Mexican. The dark-skinned man was again busy with his sweeping, but he glanced up when Nye asked in Spanish, "Who's Maria stayin' with, Benito?"

The Mexican shrugged.

Also in Spanish, Roderick said, "I only want to talk to her. She might do some good for my brother. And Lerraza."

Shaking his head, the janitor continued working. Roderick turned on his heel. Nye followed him to the door.

"You walk slow," the lawman said. "There's been enough trouble around here already."

"I was jumped for trying to walk slow, Sheriff. No one else is going to jump me in this town."

He hesitated in the doorway, fully expecting Nye to snap back at him. But Nye remained quiet and stiff-faced, absently fingering his scraggly mustache. Roderick stepped onto the boardwalk.

A careful man, Roderick decided, one smart enough not to stick his neck out too far for any stranger. Yet that lone judgment didn't completely satisfy Roderick. The sheriff knew his presence had contained the mob following the fight, but then he'd lapsed into a negativeness that had dejection in it. It was almost as if Nye felt shame about something. He hadn't tried to offer any excuses, nor reasons for or against what had happened. He was simply factual and that was that.

Roderick walked straight across Center towards the Shiloh Hotel. Aware that everyone in sight watched him, he deliberately moved at a slow pace. He felt more than just a stubborn purpose now, more of a rising anger that made him want them all to see who he was.

Back in his room he emptied Charlie's valise on the bed and went through the contents: a holstered Navy-issue Colt, with gunbelt wrapped carefully around it, a worn shirt, a pair of levis, heavy stockings—nothing that gave him any information. He stared at the clothing, frowning thoughtfully.

A knock on the door broke into his thoughts. Quickly he stepped to the right of the door. "Yes."

"It's Bainbridge. I've got warm water for you to clean up."

Roderick opened the door. The fat hotelman entered and placed a bucket and towel he held on the dresser. When Roderick took off his shirt, Bainbridge saw the purplish bruises on his body, and the torn skin where the Colt's barrel had struck his arm.

Bainbridge whistled softly but said nothing. While Roderick wiped the dirt-streaked blood from his mouth and face, he watched quietly. Shortly, he offered, "You won't be safe around here. Not after lickin' Moe Duff."

"I didn't give him a licking."

"You're still standin', so you won," said Bainbridge soberly. "But, he'll come after you."

Roderick dropped the soiled towels into the water bucket. "I figured he would."

"He might not use his fists next time." Bainbridge paused. "You might do right just to stay in here till your business is settled."

"That's just what some people want me to do." Roderick took a slow breath, then exhaled wearily. "The only way I'm going to find out why is to keep in the open where they can come after me."

Inside the Silver Dollar there was a lot of talk, the bar throbbing with noise. A hazy thickness of smoke hung between the shaded lamps and the tops of cowhands' sombreros and flat-crowned hats. Men draped the length of the bar and at the tables discussed loudly the fight between Roderick and the blacksmith, but Curly Gromm, standing at the window, paid no attention to the conversations.

Everyone took it as simply a grudge fight, Curly knew. Dan Wayne had been smart to have Duff take the first crack at discouraging Roderick from digging too deeply into the lynching of his brother. But Duff had failed, and it was in his hands from here on.

"What now?" Stewart asked from beside him.

"Just shut up and wait." The cowhand's flat drawl showed irritation. "He'll be out."

"Mebbe I should go around the back of the hotel. He might come out that way."

Curly wasn't listening to him. He was thinking of the bloody mess the Colt's barrel had made of Duff's head—Moe Duff, who'd taken care of ten or eleven men for Wayne, and just for a measly stinking two hundred dollars. Curly felt good. Wayne would pay a man like himself a lot more than two hundred for keeping Roderick out of his hair.

Stewart's voice broke into his thoughts. "He's comin' out, Curly. He's got his Winchester."

In a low, tense voice, "Okay . . . I see him. Don't tell the whole place."

The two men watched Roderick walk along Center and go into the livery barn. Three minutes passed before he came out, leading his black gelding. After he mounted and rode toward the Mexican section, Stewart started for the door.

"Hold it," Curly said. "He might be watchin' for you."

Stewart hesitated. "But I want to see where he's goin'."

"Damn it, give him time to clear Mex town. We'll see where he goes."

"He'll git too far ahead."

Curly walked to the batwings. He reached out with his long arm and pulled half the door back slightly so he could watch better.

After another minute, he said, "Bring the horses around back." Habitually, he hitched up his double gun rig. "Tell Ernie to keep quiet about us leavin'."

The bearded man stared at Curly's tight face. "What you goin' to do?"

"You know damned well, Harry, without me tellin' you," Curly said.

4

WILL RODERICK studied the Mexican section while he rode past. He noticed how poor each adobe was, made up mainly of waste lumber, hand-furnished bricks, and pieces of metal from flattened-out barrels, cans and discarded signs. Rusted stovepipes rose above patched roofs, or stuck out over small yards that were as shabby as the homes, designated haphazardly by a line of stones, sticks thrust into the baked flat, or a section of ragged fence here and there.

He did not miss the mute watchers in yards and doorways, nor the staring shadows behind the few unbroken windows. He'd not noticed this entering town, but now the knowledge of existing conditions accented his watchfulness. He mulled over the comparison between these hovels and the fine homes in upper Buffalo as he turned onto the prairie, riding slowly by patches of grass to the shabby acre of land near the river that the Mexicans used as a cemetery.

Roderick stopped his horse beside the lone cottonwood shading the barren soil. He sat for long moments looking at the few gravestones, makeshift crosses and numerous unmarked graves. Three which looked new enough to be Charlie's caught his eye, but he did not go close to them. There was no sense going in, not when he couldn't be sure of the grave. He was conscious of the Mexicans about the cemetery and of hidden, tense scrutiny, and it made him feel even more a stranger.

Because his brother was buried here, an empty chill had settled inside Roderick. There was six years between them. After their father died during that Texas winter of fifty-eight, Will had helped their mother bring him up. He had taught Charlie how to ride, to shoot, to fight, and had given him spending money when he had it. There were a lot of memories about Charlie, but now Roderick thought mainly of his brother's looks, the black wavy hair, white teeth, and the smooth, healthy complexion that showed through his tanned skin, and how, like any kid who'd spent most of his life along the Rio Grande, he spoke fluent Spanish.

He could understand how some people had believed Charlie was part Mexican. And, from the townspeople's behavior during the fight, he could picture how the mob had formed, what little chance Charlie must have had once they got him. About one thing he hadn't changed: mixed in with his own gnawing sense of anger in this, there was still that strong blending of stubborn belief in Roderick's mind that made him positive his brother wouldn't kill a man without being forced into it.

He pulled his horse to the left and, angling close to the line of cottonwoods and willows, followed the river, keeping far enough off to stay clear of the mosquitoes he'd struck coming in. Half an hour later, he left the trees and brush and went onto a tongue of sandbar thrusting out into the lazy current. He sat listening to the distant song of the meadowlarks as he considered what he'd learned so far. He was rubbing the black's neck while the animal drank, when the horse suddenly lifted its head, shaking drops of water from its mouth.

The gelding's ears had gone up, and the animal watched the thicket that rose across the river. Roderick stared, but could see nothing. He was not fooled, though. The black had seen or heard something.

Abruptly, acting on his experience as a soldier, he began urging the horse out of the river. In the same motion, he eased his rifle from its saddle scabbard.

Two riders broke through the willows lining the east bank. Roderick saw immediately that the bearded man was one of them. The second, tall, about his own age, wore two guns. As he pulled ahead he signaled Roderick, telling him to stay put.

Roderick controlled the urge he felt to ride on and see what would be done about it. He checked his mount, but he kept the Winchester cocked across the pommel while the newcomer's gray mare splashed toward him. At first he considered the rider to be just another working cowhand. Then a second look took in the man's hard eyes and tight mouth, and the way his right hand was poised habitually above the bone handle of his .44. Roderick raised the carbine so it pointed directly at the heart.

The rider pulled up. "Where you goin'?" he asked.

Roderick said, "You the owner of this land?"

"No. You're on Dan Wayne's spread now."

"Well, Wayne's the man I came out here to see."

The rider's cold eyes shifted from Roderick's face to the muzzle of the Winchester, then back to the purplish bruise at the corner of Roderick's mouth. Harry Stewart reined in close to the cowhand.

"You tell him to git, Curly?" Stewart asked.

Curly didn't answer. He spoke quietly to Roderick. "Mr. Wayne's laid up with a cold. He ain't seein' no visitors."

"Judge Porter seemed to think he'd see me."

"Look, I rod this spread," Curly said. "Any talkin' you do'll be to me."

Roderick backed his horse away a few steps. "First man I talk to on this ranch is the owner," he said. "I got any business with you, I'll look you up."

Stewart put in loudly, "You'd better ride back to town, Roderick. You ain't comin' in here and thinkin' . . ."

"Shut up, Harry," snapped Curly. "This is Runnin' W business. I'll handle it."

Harry Stewart began to say something, but noticing Curly's look, he remained quiet. He wiped his red sweating forehead and watched. Roderick could see now that Stewart was much younger than the beard made him seem, probably not over forty.

Curly's eyes shifted to the Winchester. "Okay, we'll ride up to the house with you." He started swinging his mare around. "We'll follow you up."

"I'll follow you," said Roderick.

Curly leaned forward, resting his arm on the saddle horn. "You talk big for a man ridin' alone where he ain't wanted."

"I learned fast not to let anyone get behind me around here."

Curly allowed him a hard grin. He signaled for Stewart to fall in alongside, and he turned his horse.

After a slight pressure from Roderick's knees the black went into motion again, following behind the others as they pushed through the brush and onto the flat. They rode in silence. Shortly, they cut onto a trail that wound across the flat and merged with a road leading to the gray ranch house and sprawling buildings of Running W. The road showed constant use by the way it was pounded down from wagon wheels and hoofs. The prairie on each side was sandy with sparse patches of sun-dried grass, not good graze land at all.

Roderick wondered about that as he studied the buildings ahead with interest. He judged that the ranch was at least six or seven years old. The house was big and sprawling, with a veranda running the length of its front. A few cottonwoods and alders and a thicker line of trees that ran along a small creek behind the house offered the ranch's only shelter. Wayne must have been certain of no Indian trouble when he'd built, for there was little effort at making Running W defensible. Roderick frowned; Wayne was a confident man—and a bit foolish, for even now there was always the threat of Indian trouble, even this deep in the Territory.

He sheathed the carbine and drew his mare up even with Curly. Together they trotted up the long drive to the veranda.

Curly's voice came presently. "You wait here," he said. "Harry'll go inside and ask if Mr. Wayne'll see you."

"Harry work here?"

Paying no attention to the question, Curly swung around and said to Harry, "You go tell Mr. Wayne we're waitin' on him."

Stewart dismounted. Roderick said, "Tell him I'll be glad to stay around a while if he wants."

Curly cleared his throat and said dryly, "If Mr. Wayne don't wanna talk, you'll go back to town."

The glance he gave then held a warning. The tall cowhand was bent forward in the saddle, his hands fingering the lariat thonged at the horn, casually, as though he were indifferent. But Roderick saw that his hidden hostility was worse than Stewart's.

A minute later, the veranda door swung open again. Stewart came out. The beard on his thin face failed to hide the look of satisfaction that was there now.

"Mr. Wayne says he'll see you in town tomorrow." He halted, once off the bottom step.

Roderick felt his anger rising. If he let them give him this runaround, he'd get nowhere. "You tell him the judge sent me?" he asked.

"He said for you to wait till he comes to town."

"You go back in and tell Wayne I'll only take a few minutes of his time," Roderick said. He leaned forward, preparing to dismount.

Stewart stepped back, startled, not expecting a turn like this. He glanced hurriedly at Curly. The tall cowhand sat his saddle easily now. He smiled, enjoying what was happening, but behind the smile was a tension that accented his threat.

"You stay right on thet horse," he said to Roderick. "You don't, you'll go back to town tied down to thet saddle."

Roderick hesitated. "My business won't take long." One boot cleared the stirrup.

Curly's right hand snapped down. His fingers were inches from the gun's bone handle when Roderick kicked the black, making it lunge forward. It smacked into Curly's mare, throwing the rider off balance. Roderick's outstretched hands locked on Curly's shoulder, gave him a savage jerk and shove, sending him smashing to the ground. He pulled his horse back, dropped his hand to his Colt.

Dazed from the fall, Curly lay sprawled in the dust. Blood oozed from his nose and scraped face. He tried to stand, but fell on his side. Then his right hand pawed for his .44.

"Go ahead," Roderick snapped coldly. "Give me a damn good reason."

"Hold it! Curly!"

The call was loud, demanding. Curly froze. Roderick glanced at the man standing in the doorway, his fleeting look getting the impression the man was old and white-haired, before his eyes returned to watching the prostrate cowhand.

"Yes, Mr. Wayne," Curly said. He'd raised up on one knee and now stood quickly.

"I'll talk to this man." Dan Wayne let the door slam shut behind him, came to the edge of the stairs, and stood staring down at Roderick. He was a gaunt, pallid man, tall and stooped, with his hands held behind his back. His brown shirt and trousers hung loosely, as if his body was simply skin and bones. There was nothing to be learned from his features as he spoke.

"Well, what do you want?"

"My name's Roderick. I'd like to talk to two of your crew. Forbes and Thompson. They said they saw my brother kill a man named Haven."

For a moment the men in front of Roderick did not

move. Then Curly, wiping blood from his jaw, said quickly, "Boss, you let me take care of this . . ."

"Shut up," Dan Wayne snapped. He'd lived in this
rough, wild land long enough to know a dangerous man
when he saw one. He watched Roderick. His voice quieted,
and he added to Stewart, "Go get Forbes and Thompson."

Stewart stared at the rancher.

"Go ahead," Wayne said. "Tell them to come here,
now."

As Stewart started across the yard toward the bunkhouse, Wayne glanced at Curly. "You see there's no trouble. We've got no quarrel with this man."

Curly's head did not turn. "I sent Thompson down to
the south pasture this mornin', Mr. Wayne. Won't be time
to git him."

Now Wayne came down to the top step. He suddenly
began coughing. When he stopped he stood there holding
one hand over his brows to shade his eyes from the glare
of the sunshine while he stared down at Roderick. His
question was low, completely honest, "You be satisfied to
talk to Forbes? He and Thompson saw the same thing,
anyway."

Roderick thought about that. They'd both have the
same story, but he wanted to look each man in the eye
when he told it. He gave his head a slow shake. "I'll talk
to Thompson later," he said.

Wayne was going to answer, but a movement near the
bunkhouse caught his attention. The door had swung open,
and Harry Stewart and a shorter, flat-faced man in shirt
sleeves were coming through the yard. Here's the show-
down, Roderick thought. Sweat was sticky beneath his
arms and across his back. A tingling sensation played with
the cramped muscles of his stomach.

When Forbes reached the steps, Wayne said, "This
man's Chico Roderick's brother. He wants to know how
Haven was killed."

Forbes said matter-of-factly, "I saw Chico and that
Mex ride off from Mike's body. They shot him and then
run off."

"Start from the beginning," Roderick told him.

Forbes flushed slightly. His look locked with Roderick's.
"Look," he said, "the boss says I tell about the killin'. But
don't you try givin' me no orders."

Roderick nodded patiently.

Dan Wayne said, "Tell him everything he wants to know." A coughing spell cut off his words, deep, throaty coughing that reddened the tight, waxen skin of his cheeks. The spell ended with long, wheezing breaths, and he spat before going on. "Start from the beginning, Dave."

The cowhand shrugged and spoke. "Me and Tommy was ridin' up from the brandin' camp. We cut onto the old stage road about a mile south of here." He stared directly into Roderick's eyes. "The three of 'em was ridin' ahead of us. They was talkin' loud, like they was arguin', when Chico drew on Haven an' shot him. I saw that, an' I'll say so in any court."

"You rode up on them, just like that?" Roderick said.

"Just like I said it."

"And it was you who took them in?"

"Was not. When they saw us comin' they rode off. Tommy chased them. I took Mike's body into Buffalo." Forbes stopped talking, then stood waiting for Roderick to speak. He felt in his back pocket and took out a plug of tobacco.

Roderick asked, "Anything else?"

Forbes bit and began chewing. "That's what I saw. That's what I'd've said in court."

"It would've been better all around if you'd had that chance in court," Roderick said.

Slowing his chewing for a moment, Forbes, his eyes narrowed under bushy black brows, stared at Roderick. "Well, you'll get the same story from Tommy," he said. "An' if you want more proof, you talk to Maria Jack."

Dan Wayne said then, "You want to wait around for Thompson to come in? I'll send Forbes out to get him." His eyes were on Forbes, warning him to keep calm.

Roderick shook his head. "I'll come out from town again. I'll finish up there and see Thompson later."

"Well, that's all, Dave," Wayne said to Forbes. Without answering, the cowhand started back toward the bunkhouse.

"You know who I'd see to find out where Maria Jack is?" Roderick said, looking at Wayne.

"I'd say any one of the Mexicans could tell you." Wayne stared bluntly at him. "Either them, or Sheriff Jaff Nye."

Roderick nodded, aware that now Harry Stewart had moved in close to him. He turned to Stewart and said easily, "I was wondering if you'd know where she is."

"How should I know?"

"You're the watch dog, aren't you?"

Stewart's eyes flicked around him. A silence fell, a taut quiet that stretched out while Curly stepped in front of Stewart. A faint warning stirred inside Roderick, making him see the threat in the tall cowhand's deliberate manner, and in Dan Wayne's watchful, hard eyes. And in the end, it was Wayne who broke the silence.

"You've no call to ride Harry, Roderick."

"He's kept a good eye on me since I got to town," Roderick said pointedly.

"Mike Haven was my friend," Stewart put in. "I . . ."

"You're welcome here to talk to Thompson when you like," Dan Wayne said again, the words falling quickly from his mouth. "You decide when to come."

"Thanks, I will," Roderick said. He saw something new in Wayne's face, something that could be only irritation, or it could be concern. He tried to keep the recognition from showing in his voice. "Probably tomorrow, Mr. Wayne."

Dan Wayne nodded, but he did not answer.

Roderick mounted the black and rode slowly along the drive. Wayne watched him, and when the rider was beyond earshot, came down the steps and stopped in front of Stewart.

"I suppose you dogged Roderick as soon as he got into town," he said. "What in hell are you doing, anyway?"

"Hell, boss, you told me to keep an eye open for him."

Wayne spat from colorless lips, saying nothing. Stewart rubbed his beard uneasily. He knew that the rancher was riled at him, and that was ominous.

"I only did what you told me, boss," he whined. "Ain't my fault he licked Moe Duff."

Frowning, Wayne looked once more toward the direction Roderick had gone. He was silent for several minutes, still watching the road.

Dan Wayne's manner was making Stewart nervous. He glanced at Curly. The tall cowhand's fingers felt the tender skin of his scraped jaw, but there was nothing to be learned from his features.

Tensely, Stewart asked, "You think he knows anythin', boss?"

"I don't know," Wayne said. "He's a cool one, though. His brother could've let him in on the whole thing. He could be troublesome."

"He can be taken care of easy enough, Mr. Wayne," Stewart offered hurriedly. "We use a knife, it'll look like a Mex did it."

Wayne stared at him. "No . . . not this time. He's got no proof about anything, even if he does know. You get into town ahead of him. Talk it up so everyone ties him up with Chico and Lerraza. Make damn sure people know he's looking for Maria, so the Mex'll be in on this."

"That's it," Stewart said, smiling broadly. He liked this much better, with a decision made and orders to follow. He began to climb onto his horse. "I'll handle it," he said. "Don't worry, boss."

"Damn it, don't call me boss."

"Sure, Dan." Stewart rode off.

After he had gone, Wayne stood silently. Curly waited. He knew, after having been with the rancher for more than seven years, that you could never guess accurately about what he was thinking or planning.

Finally Wayne said, "Follow Harry in. See he doesn't do anything to mess things up."

Curly nodded slowly.

"And check on Maria. You be sure she's careful what she says to Roderick."

"You givin' me a free hand?" Curly said flatly. "In case Roderick does find out too much?"

"Just be careful," Wayne said. "If you have to do anything, make it look like a Mex did it. There'll be enough of them who'll want first call on Roderick anyway, once they find out he only means more trouble for them."

5

THE SUN, lower above the western horizon now, hadn't lost any of its heat, though the shadows slanting east were longer and the sandbars of the Platte had lost their dazzling white glare. Roderick rode slowly, thinking, mulling over each word of the conversation at Running W. He tried to recall the expression on every face. His mind stuck on the way Stewart's look had changed when he'd called him a watch dog, and how Curly and Wayne had reacted to what was intended simply as a caustic remark.

Stewart had been watching for him all along; that was the reason he'd been so quick to pick him up talking to the Mexican boy. From now on, there was more at stake than simply clearing up Charlie's death. He could feel the threat against himself; he'd known right from the moment of tense silence that he'd buy trouble if he forced things.

He'd let it go, though. During his lifetime he had known some foolish men, a few who took unnecessary risks, believing their recklessness was courage. In most cases, he'd helped bury them.

He had time, close to three weeks more. If he asked enough questions, talked to enough people . . . if Stewart's fidgeting meant something. Being a soldier had taught Will Roderick patience. He'd done a lot of waiting in the army. He'd waited for meals, for time off, for the paymaster, even for battle. Sometimes he was bored by it, but a calm patience was the result, and he drew on that now.

The town noises came to him as he turned the gelding down the bank and into the shallow water. By crossing like this, he could enter along Buffalo's rear side and not get immediate notice. He let the black pick its own way through the sluggish channel. Once on the east bank he kept to the willow thicket, accepting the clouds of humming mosquitoes that deluged him as part of the price of returning undetected.

Roderick was surprised to learn his effort was useless. When he reined his mount out of the alley beside the hard-

36

ware store and onto Center, starting past the barber shop toward the livery, he saw how the townspeople were watching him. Men stared from the double-decked porch of the hotel. Individuals along the walks stopped to study him, while a few of the more cautious gave sneaking glances. He wondered how they had known he was coming back right now.

He had his answer then, as one face among the loungers stood out to him: Harry Stewart, his gray beard as noticeable as the "No Mex" sign nailed to the wall.

Roderick rode on, looking ahead, his hard face not changing at all.

He'd had moments like this before, one of them during the last patrol, when his company had come upon a Hunkpapa camp that they knew very well was heading north to join Sitting Bull. He'd known this same feeling then, being watched, not certain of what was coming next, but expecting the bloody battle that might follow.

Strange, he thought, that this time it felt worse, more dangerous. It was the heavy distrust that bounced from group to group, but even more the tense hate he saw in the eyes of the few Mexicans he passed before stopping the black in front of the livery.

At the water trough, Roderick dismounted.

The tall, long-faced hostler came out of the barn. "I can't handle your horse," he said bluntly.

"You took him before."

"Can't take him now," the hostler said. Two men coming along the street had stopped to watch what was going on. The hostler looked at them. He shifted his feet uneasily. His mouth tightened downward. "Got no room for another horse," he added.

Roderick glanced past the doors, seeing two empty stalls in the right hand row. "What about them?" he said, still casual.

"They're taken," the hostler answered quickly. "Look, I just work here. I can't take your mount." He eyed the spectators as though he were expecting them to say something.

Roderick gazed at the men. He saw how they watched. Both were quiet, with the same heavy distrust in their faces. They looked back at him deliberately.

"Well, I'll leave him here in case there is room," Roderick said.

The hostler stirred and spat and rubbed his face. "But my boss said . . ."

"Who's your boss?"

"Mr. Ockers at the general store."

"I'll talk to him," Roderick said. He held out the bridle.

Shaking his head, "Mr. Ockers said he don't want your horse here." His voice was definite, but worry was there. "I got my orders, mister."

Roderick knew it would not help him to pressure the man. It would only make more and bitter enemies for him. He could hear a mutter and movement beginning between the watchers. But the talk quieted when he turned and, drawing the black on its bridle after him, started from the work area.

The hostler, his complete confidence returned, took out his pipe and began filling it. He remarked to one of the watchers, "When he came in earlier, he said he wasn't a Mex. Old Man Ockers was mad as hell when he heard he was Chico's brother."

"Sure, how could you know he was lying," said the smaller of the two, a round, soft-bellied man. "I'd've taken him at his word, too."

"He came damn near costin' me my job," the hostler said. Then he cursed. "He'll find all the trouble he wants if he tries somethin' like that again."

"Damn right," the other said. "We used a rope on his brother; we can use one on him quick enough, too."

The hostler frowned knowingly. He turned and gave a steady, hard stare at Roderick, who was now halfway to the hotel.

Judge Porter usually left his office and went home long before now, but when he'd heard talk going around against Roderick, he'd decided to try straightening out the situation. He'd stood in the deep shadow of the courthouse, sweating in the dry, stifling heat that hadn't let up even though night was coming on. Despite the discomfort and the dust that spotted his black suit and fedora, he waited, for he knew exactly what he wanted to do. He'd make enemies, but someone had to stop trouble from bursting out again.

As soon as he saw Roderick leading his horse from the livery, he made his move. He went hurriedly along the walk and up onto the hotel steps. The men standing there were so intent on watching Roderick they didn't seem to notice the judge.

"What's all the commotion?" he asked one of the men.

"That stranger. One that came in today."

The judge glanced to the left. He saw that Roderick was still two blocks away. "Why is he so special?" he asked.

Harry Stewart answered that. "You know why, Judge," he said. "You was talkin' to him. You know he's Chico's brother."

When the bearded man finished speaking, everyone was silent, even the men just joining the group. All waited to see what the judge would say. Some had been down on him since he'd sentenced the leaders of the lynch mob to three years, but he had the final say on the law in this county, and they waited to hear what line he'd take.

Judge Porter said, "Harry, you can't hold that man responsible for what Chico did."

"Hell, Judge," a voice from the rear of the porch called, "you know how we're handlin' them Mexes. And this one's taken a room here at the hotel. I say he's gotta be taught a lesson."

"Roderick's not a Mexican."

"What you talkin' about? He's Chico's brother, ain't he?"

The judge felt the hostility, heard the low murmur starting. The talk died when he shook his head. "I've got Roderick's birth certificate and papers from the army. He isn't Mexican. And neither was Chico." Now, he looked directly at Bainbridge, the fat hotel man. "I wouldn't put him out of his room, if I were you."

Stewart glared at the judge. "Whatcha givin' us? Everyone knows Chico was part Mex. It's easy for that stranger to lie about . . ."

"I've sent to Texas for a record of Chico's birth, and to Fort Abe Lincoln, so I can verify Roderick's story. You let me handle this, Harry." The judge looked again to the left and saw he still had another few seconds. "Anyone who causes unnecessary trouble I'll have in my court. Remember that, all of you."

The gaunt cheeks above Stewart's beard began to turn red. There was a low muttering that quieted as soon as it broke out, leaving a tense uneasiness behind. One or two of the men stepped off the porch and went their way, and, shortly, alone or in pairs, others followed. Those who remained kept watching Roderick.

Stewart said nothing. He waited until Roderick reached the hitchrail and stopped. Then, he swung around, pushed past the few remaining men, and stomped into the lobby.

In the silence, Judge Porter said, "Sergeant, I've got plenty of extra room in my barn, if you'd like to leave your horse there."

Roderick nodded. He gave no notice to Stewart's actions. There was a questioning frown on his face as he looked up at Bainbridge. "This isn't your battle," he said flatly. "You might be smart to put my roll out in the lobby."

"Why should I," the fat man said, "unless you got no money to pay."

Will Roderick merely studied Bainbridge's face. He'd known the hotel man had tried to help from the start, but he was unsure how he'd react once out-and-out hostility got to himself. A man could lose enthusiasm for bucking any crowd if his business would suffer.

Now, as if there was no more to say, Bainbridge swung his bulk around and started inside.

"You see, Sergeant," said Judge Porter, "there are plenty of people here who are willing to forget."

"How about Stewart's kind?"

"In time they'll change, too." The judge came down the steps and into the street.

Roderick glanced into the hotel. He saw the hazy outline of Stewart's bony figure watching him, the bearded face hidden in the shadows. Roderick peered through the doorway another long moment before he gently tugged at the bridle and fell in alongside the judge.

Inside the hotel, Harry Stewart made a straight course to the desk. He halted directly opposite Bainbridge. The obese clerk had the ledger open and was again looking at Roderick's signature.

"You really gonna let him stay here?" Stewart asked.

"Why not?" Bainbridge said. "You heard the judge. He ain't a Mex."

"Maybe there's people who don't care if he's Mex or not."

"Meanin' Dan Wayne?" The round face came up then, and the deep-set eyes had a knowing look in them. "You know, Harry, this is one buildin' Wayne don't own. You can check out of here if you don't like how things are run."

Stewart said matter-of-factly, "There are times when you're hard to get along with. It ain't good to be a troublemaker."

"Lettin' a soldier on leave hire one of my rooms ain't bein' a troublemaker." The knowing expression was still there, but it had hardened. "Unless there's people who're afraid he'll make trouble for them. I suppose then I'd be kind of a troublemaker."

Harry Stewart forced a laugh. "What trouble could he make?"

"You so sure he can't make any?"

Stewart didn't answer. Frowning, he turned and went down the corridor to his room. He swore softly to himself as he unlocked the door and entered.

The door closed behind him, and in the darkness he heard a chair creak and footsteps creaking the floor.

"What the . . ."

A match sparkled and the lamp above the bed flooded the room with yellow light. Stewart blinked and saw Moe Duff standing beside the iron-posted bed. A thick white bandage covered the huge man's forehead, but it didn't hide the swelling there, or the bruised discoloring over his eyes.

"Where's my money?" Duff asked.

"Money? What money?"

Duff glowered, flexing his thick arms like a fighter getting ready. "Two hundred dollars. That's what I want."

"Well, I . . ." Stewart shifted nervously, glanced towards the door.

"Two hundred." The blacksmith moved fast, blocking off any escape. He pointed to his bandaged head. "I got this for two hundred."

Harry Stewart's voice was pinched with fright. Then, he started for the hall. "I'll see Curly. He'll . . ."

Duff stopped his words with a savage backhanded blow that knocked the bearded man over the bed.

Stewart pulled himself to his feet, careful to keep the bed between himself and Duff. There was blood at the corner of his mouth, a thin trickle of red that ran into his beard.

"I ain't got your money," he cried, dabbing one hand

at the blood on his lip. "Mr. Wayne said you don't get it because you didn't finish Roderick."

"I fought him. That's all I said I'd do."

"He said you hadda finish him."

Duff regarded Stewart impassively. "He wants me to finish him, I'll finish him." He stepped forward. "Give me your gun."

Stewart jerked back, terrified. He quickly pulled his Colt from its holster and held it out.

Taking it, Duff pointed to the window. "You come out this way with me. I want Wayne to know for sure it was me who did it."

"No. Mr. Wayne don't want the ranch connected to Roderick."

"Ain't no one gonna see me when I get him."

"But Mr. Wayne said . . ."

The protest was shut up as Duff shoved Stewart hard across the room, slamming him into the wall.

"Open that window. Start out."

Stewart obeyed, and when he had dropped to the ground, Duff blew out the wall lamp and followed.

6

WILL RODERICK deliberately walked at a slow pace, past the white-painted, substantial houses of upper Buffalo. The sunset reflected from the large glass doors in a blaze of orange and red, and already bright and shining lamps burning on front porches lightened the rising first gray of nightfall. Roderick ignored those who watched from their porches, looking ahead as he waited for the judge to speak.

Harry Stewart had been told to make things rough for him, or scare him. Whatever the reason, when they decided to crowd him they were worried. Up to the present, Roderick had still had a doubt. Now the doubt was gone. There was a lot more to be learned about the killing of Haven and the lynching; but how did he go about getting them?

Finally he asked Judge Porter, "Did Mike Haven have any connection with my brother . . . work with him or anything?"

"No. He worked for the freight line. Chico did business with him, but that's all that was between them that I know of."

"How about Harry Stewart? He have any business with Charlie?"

"Not that I knew about. Why?"

"I think Stewart was watching for me, by the way he tagged onto me as soon as I hit town."

Judge Porter nodded, admitting the possibility. "I'll be frank," he said, an uneasy shadow falling across his face. "The people who hated your brother are talking against you. Be careful until you leave town."

"Doesn't it seem odd they'd be stirred up so fast?"

The judge was thoughtful. "It isn't just men who liked Mike Haven," he said shortly. "It's the Mexicans, too. All their trouble started because of Chico. Now that the word has spread about your being here, they could be troublesome."

"Lerraza was a Mex, and he ran. Remember, Charlie didn't run."

43

"Sergeant," the judge said with concern, "try to understand Stewart and men like him. Don't let them push you. We don't want another lynching here."

"I'm not planning to kill anyone, Judge."

"I wasn't worrying about that. But I know how fast a lynch mob can get formed." The statement was made in a slow, grave voice.

There was a tightening at the corners of Roderick's mouth. He remained silent.

They were almost to the Porter home. The judge peered towards the long veranda, his eyes troubled. "I spoke to Sheriff Nye about you a little while ago, Sergeant. He said you could move into the jail if there's any trouble."

Will Roderick checked the irritation he felt. He did not say anything for a few moments. He welcomed the judge as a sympathizer, but this kind of help would only hurt in the end. He said, "I don't think there's all the danger you believe there is."

"Think about it, anyway. Your living at the jail can do a lot to keep trouble from starting."

Roderick's face was sober with thought. As they turned into the judge's drive, the sound of a chair scraping the veranda floor came from above. The rustle of starched clothing followed, and Mrs. Porter's thin, impatient face peered down at them from behind the morning-glory vines, her chilly eyes over the high-arched nose sighted directly on her husband.

Judge Porter strained at politeness. "You remember Sergeant Roderick," he said.

Her lips tightened as her gaze shifted to Roderick, and with a flicker returned to the judge.

"I'd like to talk to you inside, Judge Porter," she said.

"I'll be in shortly, Alma. Just as soon as I show the sergeant where to put his horse."

Mrs. Porter's face was accusingly direct. "What I have to say won't wait," she said.

As though the matter were settled, she swung around and walked to the opposite end of the porch. Turning again, she stared back at her husband.

The judge looked at Roderick. "Take any stall you'd like. I'll come back in a few minutes."

"Don't bother, Judge. I'll just give him a rub and then go along."

"Well, I'll try to get back there," the judge said. He

crossed the lawn to the porch steps. He saw the furious expression on his wife's face.

"Why did you bring that man back to this house?" she snapped.

"He's not going to stay here, Alma. I'm just letting him use the barn for his horse."

"Why?"

"They wouldn't let him use the livery." He added gravely, "I had to do something, Alma. He's not the type man who'll stand being humiliated. I had to do something to stop the trouble."

"Trouble is just what that man will bring to this house. You go out back and tell him to take his animal elsewhere."

Her eyes stared directly into the judge's face. He looked away, lifted an unsteady hand to rub his chin.

"I can't send him away. I've told him he can use the barn."

"Either you tell him, or I will, Judge Porter."

The thin white lines in the judge's face seemed to darken slightly as he flushed. He studied his wife's face, visibly bracing himself. "I can't," he said. "I've done enough in this whole rotten mess. I won't do anything to make things worse now."

Will Roderick had put his gelding into the stall closest to the barn door. He was almost finished rubbing the animal down when a black surrey swung into the drive and came straight to the barn. He turned and saw Lucy Porter watching him from where she sat on the stuffed leather seat.

"Hello," she called when still a few yards away. She was smiling, recognition in her eyes.

Roderick touched his hat. "Hello, Miss Porter," he said politely. And, gesturing at the team, "I'll handle them for you."

Her enthusiasm checked, she looked at him strangely. "You're living at the hotel?"

"Yes."

She pointed back toward the house. "I thought Uncle might offer you a room here. It might be better for you that way."

"Why shouldn't I stay at the hotel?"

Her face was grave. "You'll be here only a short time.

And since Uncle is handling your business, I . . . There's so much talk against you." She shivered. "I can feel how much some people here hate you."

"No matter what's being said, their talk isn't going to hurt me."

"But it's something that can get to be worse than just talk. It could . . . they lynched Chico out of hate, and now all that's growing against you."

She glanced over her shoulder to the house. Roderick's directness bothered her. Now that she thought about it, she remembered that she had felt this same manner about him in the hallway when she'd opened the door. There was an honesty, a sincerity to it that had made her feel close to him from the start, and somehow afraid of him, too.

"I should go inside," she said, as she began getting down. Roderick took her arm, letting it go when she stepped onto the ground.

"How long will you stay here after the will is settled?" she asked.

"I'm not sure yet." He waited for her to move toward the porch, but she kept watching him.

"I'm sorry Chico was your brother," she said in a low tone.

"Charlie was a good brother, Miss Porter."

"I mean I'm sorry he was hanged. It was a terrible thing."

He stared at her, puzzled. "You didn't see it, did you?"

She shook her head. "We heard all the shouting, but we didn't know until it was all over." Intently, she studied his face. "I'm very sorry. I was hoping you'd come back so I could tell you."

Roderick nodded gratefully. He opened his mouth to reply, then stopped when he heard the back door to the house open.

Mrs. Porter came out first. When she saw the surrey the harsh lines returned to her jaw and nose. She stopped on the small back porch next to the icebox. The judge halted beside her.

"Sergeant Roderick offered to unhitch the team," Lucy said, her look bright.

"The judge will handle that, dear," said Mrs. Porter.

"I'll be glad to do it," Roderick said.

"No. The judge will do it."

In the short silence, Roderick and the girl exchanged

quick glances. Then, Lucy said, "Auntie, you know it's too much for Uncle."

The older woman's stare didn't leave the girl's face. "Because Judge Porter does business with this man, it doesn't mean we must associate with him." She eyed Roderick from behind her web of wrinkles. "I didn't want my husband to have anything to do with that murderer's will. I still don't."

Roderick did not speak. He heard the judge say, "Now, Alma, the sergeant had nothing to do . . ."

"I'll thank you to keep your business in your office, Judge Porter." Her words snapped out at the man, taking all authority from him.

Lucy stared, dumbfounded. The judge came down the steps and stopped at the surrey.

The silence stretched out until Mrs. Porter said, "Come along, Lucy." She pulled open the door and went inside.

"I'm sorry, Sergeant. You still leave your horse here," Judge Porter said calmly, but a slight flush was burning around his ears. He took Lucy's arm.

Will Roderick caught the girl's modified glance, and he tipped his hat, nodding understandingly. The girl, still embarrassed, went up onto the porch with the judge.

Roderick stood watching until the door closed behind them. Then he finished rubbing down the gelding and after that forked some fresh hay into the bin. He was thinking of Lucy, the friendliness of her talk, the sincerity in her pretty face, but there was nothing careless about him. That is why he caught the slight hint of movement when it came from somewhere beyond the barn door.

It was only the snapping of a twig, but instantly he lunged away from the horse and into the shadows of the stall, drawing his Colt as he moved.

7

FOR a long moment Roderick stood there staring beyond the open barn door. He had no idea who was there, nor did he have any illusions about himself. Feeling against him filled the air in the town, from the Mexicans as well as from the whites. His being killed would settle a lot of problems that had come up since this afternoon.

"Señor Roderick? You there, Señor Roderick?"

A small form was silhouetted in the lamplight from the judge's back porch. Roderick could make out the smooth oval face of the Mexican boy he'd talked to when he'd ridden in.

Relief made his stomach weak. He slid the Colt back into its holster, then said, "What do you want, kid?"

The boy's head jerked around at the shadowed bin. "I come from Maria Jack," he said in a low, nervous voice. "You were asking for her?"

"Yes."

"She wants to see you."

"Where is she?"

Now the boy glanced back toward the street. Just as quickly he looked into the house, as if fearing someone would surprise him.

"Maria wants you to come now. In five, six minutes, come past the livery. I'll meet you and take you to her."

"The sheriff tell her I was looking for her?"

The boy did not answer the question. He said, "Come alone, señor. You do not tell the sheriff."

"I'll be there."

The boy turned and started away, his bare feet pattering on the hard ground. Roderick leaned closer to the door and watched the boy's small form become a vague shadow in the darkness. Then he turned out of sight around the corner of the barn.

Roderick made a final hasty check of his gelding, seeing he would be comfortable and well fed. In the darkness he stood motionless, a tense worried feeling within him. There might be more to this than simply talking to Maria Jack, he knew. Anyone could have sent the boy, anyone could be setting him up for something.

Again his hand touched his holstered gun, easing it a bit before he closed the barn behind him and went along the driveway.

The town was rather quiet, aside from the tinkle of a piano mixed with the talk and occasional laughter from the saloons. A slight evening breeze coming off the river already made the air comfortably cool.

Roderick paused at an intersection, waiting until a carriage moved sedately past. People along the street stood out plainly in the lamplight and bright full moon.

Not hurrying, he angled across Center and stepped onto the walk in front of the millinery. Ahead, on the hotel steps, the short, paunchy figure of Bainbridge appeared. The hotelman waved to Roderick.

"I've been waitin' for you," he said when Roderick reached him. "I figure you must be hungry by now." He took hold of Roderick's arm. "I've got some steak waitin' inside."

"I'll take you up on that in a little while. Right now . . ."

The fat man protested. "You shouldn't be out alone like this." He tugged at the arm to get Roderick moving.

Roderick stood still. "I've got to stay out here for awhile. Alone."

"Not in the dark. Not unless you want to commit suicide."

Bainbridge tugged at the arm again, and Roderick walked with him into the lobby. Bainbridge paused to glance back out into the street.

"You know what a damn easy target you made out there?" he asked.

Roderick merely nodded. Bainbridge had done him more of a favor than he realized. He gazed thoughtfully into the man's face.

"Is there a back door into the alley?"

"In the kitchen."

"Will you do something for me?"

Bainbridge's face changed, becoming cautious. "Anythin' short of handlin' a gun. I ain't a match for anyone in this town when it comes to gunplay."

"You only have to go into my room," Roderick told

him. "Light the lamp so anyone watching will think I'm there."

"Sure." Bainbridge went along the hallway.

For another minute Roderick stood still, until Bainbridge had the lamp going inside his room. Then he hurried through the kitchen and stepped carefully out into the alleyway.

He moved noiselessly past the buildings that fronted on Center Street. He felt himself get tense once he was even with the livery, and, as if habitually, he slowed his step before turning into the darkened alley. From somewhere ahead in Mexican Town the faint, lazy sound of a guitar came to him. He went on, having no certainty he was doing right. He turned into the alley and slid along close to the side of the barn.

"Señor . . . Señor Roderick?"

Roderick crouched like a cat, pulled his gun as he pressed close to the rough boards of the building. He knew the Mexican boy's voice, but he had to be sure. Fear held him, running up his back, prickling his muscles.

The boy's voice again came out of the thin, threatening silence. "Señor Roderick?"

"Yes."

Now the dark-skinned youth slid in beside him. "I look for you to come by street, señor." His glance was on the Colt. "I'll go first," he said.

Ashamed at letting the boy see his distrust, Roderick holstered the gun.

The youth led him back to the alley's rear and past the corral, then made his way among the closest of the shanties, where the shadowed dimness of the moonlight made everything barely visible. The air was heavy with the mixed smells of burned oil, and sweat, and Mexican cooking. Roderick cautiously watched the shadows as he followed, his long frame bent over to dodge jutting stovepipes, and he slowed often so not to trip over the stick fences and large whitewashed rocks that defined the yards. Finally they came to a stop at a well-kept shack. The boy knocked gently.

Inside a slow footstep sounded, shuffling on the sand floor. And shortly a whisper came. "You, Tonio . . . you?"

"Sí."

The door opened. A small, thin Mexican looked out. He

kept the lamp he held well clear of his face so the smoke would be out of his eyes.

"You go, Tonio," he said. He stood back to let Roderick enter.

Roderick removed his sombrero and stepped through the doorway. He stopped short and let his hand brush the butt of his Colt when he saw more Mexicans were standing inside the small room. Four were young, the fifth an aged man.

"Señor, you are in no danger," the man holding the lamp said in English. He was middle-aged, rather light-skinned. Roderick could see some scars on his face when he bent to place the lamp on the table. "You want to talk to Maria Jack?"

"Yes." He made no pretense at hiding the hand on the gun.

"She will come, señor."

One of the others, a tall, greasy-faced young man, said, "Hai, Tobrez, you are a fool to trust this gringo."

Tobrez looked at him. "Silence, Ramon. Did not Jalisca and I agree on this?"

"But you know nothing about him. How can you be sure of him?"

Tobrez did not answer. He said to Roderick, "You were at jail today. You said you would help Lerraza?"

"Yes. If I can." Roderick was going to say more, but a knock at the door stopped him.

The Mexicans went into action immediately, breaking up their group. Tobrez walked to the door. The others stepped quickly behind a large multicolored Sioux blanket hanging across the back half of the room. Roderick saw now that the young men had held guns out of sight all along.

In his own tongue, Tobrez asked, "Who is it?"

A low, muffled answer came. Tobrez opened the door and stood talking to someone outside for a few moments. When he closed the door, the others reappeared.

Tobrez spoke to Ramon. "You get Maria now," he said. Then, turning to the old man, he said, "Roderick was not followed, Jalisca. For me, I think it is all right."

"We shall see, amigo," the man named Jalisca answered.

He came forward to the table. Roderick could see him clearly in the lamplight. His coffee-colored face showed nothing, but there was all the unbreakable spirit and patience of his people in his eyes as he watched Tobrez, waiting for him to speak.

To Roderick, Tobrez said, "Chico was living here almost two years. You knew that?"

Roderick nodded. "Last time I heard from him was the middle of last year. He said he planned to stay in this town for good."

"And you knew what he did here?"

"Only that he was in business for himself. His letter didn't say much."

Tobrez glanced at Jalisca. Roderick caught the look that passed between them, but it didn't tell him anything.

One of the young men said, "You let him know how Chico was. How it was for the money he bring us all this trouble."

When one or two of the others joined in, muttering loudly, Tobrez snapped, "Silence! You know this is the only way."

Roderick asked, "What's he driving at, Tobrez?"

In the tense quiet that followed, Roderick felt the young men close in on him. If trouble came, fighting would do no good. He placed both hands flat on the round wooden table for all to see plainly.

Finally, Tobrez said, "You know that Pablo Lerraza worked for Chico?"

"Yes."

"Pablo was handyman," Tobrez said. "He clean, keep everything fixed in cantina and hotel. Anything Chico tell him to do. When boxes come from freight line this day, he open them. Guns were inside, señor. Many guns."

Surprise showed on Roderick's face. "Say it straight, Tobrez."

"Chico was smuggling guns, señor. Six boxes come for him that day. He mad at Lerraza for opening boxes. And when Haven come from freight office asking about boxes, he and Chico argue."

Smuggling . . . that stung, but it was said so honestly, Roderick remained calm. "Can you prove all this?" he said.

"Sí. Lerraza saw the guns. Maria, too. Both heard what Haven say. And, Lerraza rode out to Wayne's ranch with . . ."

"What's Wayne got to do with this?"

"He owns the freight line. Haven only run it for him. Chico went to ranch to talk to Wayne. On the way back, Haven and Chico fight. Chico kill Haven."

"Lerraza saw the killing?"

Tobrez nodded. "He was right behind them. But he had no part in killing."

"But he ran. Why, when Charlie didn't?"

The little Mexican was silent in the low grumbling that came from the younger men. When he spoke, the watchers quieted.

"A rabbit runs for the hole when he hears the coyote, señor. Lerraza saw the mob take Chico. He knew he too would be hung. Our people hid him until he got away to Mexico."

Now the mumbling was renewed. Tobrez glanced at the other Mexicans, but if he had anything to say to them, he changed his mind. He shrugged his shoulders before he went on, as if at some thought of his own. "We had hoped you would know something to help Lerraza. But . . ."

Roderick broke in. "Why didn't he tell all that to the sheriff? Or to the judge?"

"Señor, Chico was lynched because he was so close to our race . . . and all this trouble has followed." Tobrez's voice sounded hollow. "Lerraza would've been a fool to stay here with the mob after him."

Roderick leaned forward, close to Tobrez. He saw a glint of lamplight reflecting on a knife or gunbarrel, but he paid no attention. He'd seen enough Hunkpapas, Ogallalas, Brules and other tribes of the Sioux with Henry or Winchester rifles to know smuggling was going on. But he wanted more proof before he'd be convinced Charlie had a part in it.

"Would Lerraza come back here?" he said. "If I can get the judge to . . ."

He stopped talking in that moment, when he heard the door open. All heads turned. The Mexicans brandished their guns. Roderick saw the girl then, standing there in the shadows of the threshold beside the man called Ramon. She came forward slowly. Once she was in the flickering light, Roderick could see the reddish bruise that discolored the left side of her face, and her cut, puffed lips.

Ramon said, "I find her like this, Tobrez. She was lying in Jalisca's garden."

Tobrez said, "Who did it, Maria?"

She shook her head and said through swollen lips, "From behind, someone hit me." She trembled, as though suddenly chilled. Her silver earrings shuddered in the light.

"Was it a gringo?"

"I do not know." Maria glanced around at the faces, finally stopping at Roderick. "You want to talk," she asked.

To Roderick, her stare showed nothing, a complete lack of consciousness of pain, or hate, or excitement. She had long black hair, and she wore a low-cut white blouse and flowered cotton skirt that showed the lovely lines of her body. She realized he was taking her measure, but it didn't seem to bother her.

Roderick asked, "Who'd want to beat you like that?"

Not answering, Maria simply watched him, and he knew she was still stunned. He heard the dim mumbling begin around him.

He said, "You were at the cantina the afternoon Haven was killed?"

"Yes."

"You heard the argument?"

"About the guns . . . they argued. Chico was mad at Haven for sending the guns to the cantina. Then they went to Running W to settle the trouble."

"What happened to the guns, Maria?"

Tiredly, "Man named Stewart from the freight line came for them. He . . ."

"Harry Stewart?"

"Yes. He drive wagon for freight line."

He nodded. That was Stewart's connection to Wayne. The bearded man's waiting and watching, the hate he'd shown. It all had to be tied into something deeper than just driving a freight wagon for Wayne. It was little enough to go on, but it was all he had. He'd have his talk with Stewart now. The trick was to get him alone.

Roderick said to Maria, "Where'll you be if I want to talk to you again?"

"I am at Jalisca's." She looked at Jalisca, and the old man nodded.

"No. That's not right," Ramon said. "This gringo comes again it will only make more trouble for us." The other young men joined in the protest.

Roderick watched them, hearing the cursing against the

man they called Chico. Roderick straightened his body rigidly. He looked about, felt the hate in each answering glare.

With a single gesture, Tobrez silenced them, and said to Roderick, "You can talk to Maria here. There'll be no danger to Jalisca. But do not hope for Lerraza to return. He'll never come back here, señor."

Roderick nodded. He turned and walked across the dirt floor and, opening the door, started out.

The shots came in that moment his body was etched clearly in the lamplight. Two shots, so quick in succession they sounded as one. His hat was torn from his head. The bullets smashed resoundingly into the door.

It took a fraction of a second for Roderick to drop flat, draw his gun.

"The lamp . . . douse the lamp," he yelled back to Tobrez. And, as complete darkness came, he was moving forward, heading for the closest cover.

8

Roderick reached a small shed and crouched behind it. He peered ahead and on both sides. With the moonlight blocked by the bunched shanties, he could see only night, but he caught the confusion of heavy running to his left . . . away from him.

He fired once, into the air, hoping to draw his enemy's fire. Then he was in motion again, moving after the clomping of the footsteps.

At the corner of a shack he halted and edged around cautiously. Fifty feet ahead, the dark forms of two running men were clear in a patch of smoky lamplight beaming from a window. One huge, his wide shoulders stooped as he ran, the other taller, but too far away to judge at all.

Moe Duff for one, he was sure.

Roderick fired twice, aiming low so a bullet wouldn't ricochet into one of the shacks.

A quick yell of pain bellowed out of the blank darkness ahead, followed immediately by the heavy thump of a falling body. Roderick crouched, kept advancing. Two . . . two . . . his brain kept repeating . . . there were two of them.

Yells came from all directions, calls and questions in excited Spanish. The sound of bare feet was loud around Roderick, making it seem that all of Mexican Town was boiling out, terrified, everyone heading for the shooting.

Close by, a woman called shrilly and a child's voice answered. Suddenly, behind her, someone lighted a lamp, and, just as foolishly dangerous, another one went on. A savage thrust of fear drove through Roderick, silhouetted himself now.

He could see Duff plainly in the new lamplight. The blacksmith lay prone; his immense body was writhing in the dust as he grasped at his right thigh. Roderick pressed close to the damp wall of a shack, cursing as he pictured the second bushwhacker concealed in the shadows beyond Duff.

But no more shots came.

Roderick let out a long breath. For a moment he

watched Duff. The blacksmith was letting out a steady stream of obscenity at Roderick.

"Get up," Roderick said, stepping closer to Duff. "Get up slowly."

Duff stared hatefully at Roderick. His wide face, white with pain, was made even whiter somehow by the bandage circling his forehead. He rolled to the left, as though he meant to stand, but instead he came up with a Colt.

"Two hundred dollars, Roderick," he cried. "That's what you're worth to me."

Roderick's leg shot out, his booted foot catching Duff in the pit of his stomach. The Colt went skidding along the ground. Duff crashed back, groveled in the dust. Roderick stood over him.

"Who put you on me?" he asked. From around the corner of a shack he saw a Mexican man appear. Then two more men. They carried carbines, held them ready. "Duff, who put you on me?"

"Why should I tell you?" Duff spat.

"It'll go easier on you."

Duff cursed. He shifted his weight so he rested on the good leg, then began to sit up. Roderick holstered his gun.

Duff rolled fast to the right, his hairy arm reaching out in the movement, grasping the Colt from the dirt and cocking it as he brought it up into Roderick's chest.

"Two hun—" was all he said before Roderick's quick-drawn six-shooter blasted two holes that punctured his chest and ripped clear through the thick body. Duff flopped back and lay still.

More Mexicans crowded into the alleyway. The men who'd seen the shooting gaped, frozen. Most of the others were simply confused, and they chattered loudly. One or two stood stiff-legged while they stared around as though they'd just wakened and didn't have an idea what to do next.

In Mexican, someone called loudly, "The sheriff's coming." The mob crowded in closer together. The talk died.

Roderick was holstering his gun when Sheriff Nye appeared. The slim-shouldered lawman and three heavily armed cowhands close behind him pushed their way through the crowd. Roderick gazed down at Duff. He'd never understand what made a man kill for money. The two hundred dollars had changed this man into a beast. He'd done his best not to kill Duff. The person who really killed him was the one who'd put up the bounty. And that man would still be around with his money.

Nye saw Roderick immediately. He gestured with the short-barreled riot gun he held for those in close to move back. One glance at the body on the ground, and his expression stiffened. He stopped short and picked up Duff's gun.

"He tried to get you?" he said to Roderick.

Roderick nodded, looking at the dead man. "He wanted it that way," he said.

"*Si*," a short, dark Mexican said. "I see it all. This man have to kill." The men standing beside him echoed the words.

Sheriff Nye wasn't looking at the Mexicans. His mouth beneath the scraggly mustache was tight, and his eyes were worried as he surveyed the spectators.

The Mexican named Tobrez stepped in close to Nye. "I see the shooting begin," he said. "Blacksmith bushwhacked to start it."

"There were two of them," said Roderick. "One got away."

"You recognize him?"

"Too dark. It could've been anyone in town."

"Yeah," a beefy, whiskered cowhand behind Nye said sarcastically, "could've been a Mex as well as anybody."

With that, Ramon and some of the other young Mexicans began muttering. Nye looked around slowly, letting his gaze slide over their faces.

His eyes stopped on Roderick. "I'll take your story in my office," he said.

"I'll only repeat what I've said, Sheriff."

"You were the one they shot at . . . right?"

"Yes."

"You come along with me, anyway." Nye glanced at one of the men who had begun grumbling in a low voice. The Mexican grew silent.

The whiskered cowhand behind Nye spoke up. "How about all the guns these Mex got," he said. "They ain't supposed to have guns." He held his Winchester hip-high, as though he expected to use it.

The watchers were so quiet now that the small shuffling of boots sounded loud. Nye gave a warning look to the man who'd spoken, and then he swung his eyes back to Tobrez.

"You get these people inside," he ordered. "Make sure they stay inside the rest of the night."

"Sí," Tobrez said.

The sheriff swung around and spoke loudly. "All right," he said, "break it up."

The watchers began moving. When the last Mexican turned away, Nye made a sign to Roderick with his hand and started back toward the street.

Once out on Center, they saw the townspeople out in front of their homes talking, serious-faced people who craned their necks to see what was going on. A crowd had gathered in front of the jail. More were joining all the time, coming along the walks and the middle of the street. Before Roderick stepped into the sheriff's office, he caught sight of Judge Porter making his way from upper Buffalo. He was running, with his black coat flapping behind him.

The excitement had gone through everyone. A skinny old man in faded blue workclothes, and with a long, narrow snub-nosed head, called above the talk to the sheriff.

"Heard them Mex got after Chico's brother," he rasped. He made his voice louder once he saw he held the center of attention. "That right, hey?"

Sheriff Nye halted in the doorway. He stared at the crowd. "Moe Duff tried to kill Roderick. The Mexicans had nothing to do with it."

"They bringin' Moe up now," someone called. "They be a trial, Jaff?"

"It was self-defense," Nye said quietly. He watched the faces, aware of the low talk running through the crowd.

"But them Mex was all out with guns," the old man said. "That's what I heard."

A new voice broke in. "How about that? Them Mex is carryin' guns now. They ought to be taken care of, Sheriff."

Nye said calmly, "You forget anythin' like that."

"Why should we?" Harry Stewart called.

The sheriff swung fully around. His hard stare searched for Stewart in the rear of the crowd. "There'll be no one goin' after the Mex," he said tightly. "I'll hear no more talk of trouble from any of you."

Stewart began to sputter, but when the sheriff looked levelly into his eyes, the sputter died.

"Now, break this up," Nye said. His voice was hoarse

and tense. He waited there in the doorway, still watching Stewart.

Harry Stewart stood silent for a minute, as if considering the order carefully. Finally he turned away from the sheriff's belligerent look. He took just three steps before he noticed that Curly had been standing a little way behind him all along.

He hesitated, and then stopped walking. "You in town, Curly? I didn't know . . ." He paused.

Curly shifted his weight. He glanced back toward the sheriff's office.

Stewart grimaced. "Duff was a damned fool to try gettin' Roderick that way," he said.

Curly had seen Stewart running up from lower Buffalo just after the shooting. The tall cowhand grabbed the grinning man's coat sleeve and yanked him to one side, so they were clear of listeners.

His voice pitched low, Curly snapped, "What in hell you tryin' to do? Get them Mex workin' with Roderick?"

"Hell, I just . . ."

"You were with Duff down there."

"I couldn't get out of it, Curly. Moe was killin' mad. He forced me to go with him."

"You git out to Runnin' W. Tell Mr. Wayne what happened down in Mex Town."

"But, what about Rod . . ."

A slight raising of one hand brought silence. Beneath his Stetson's shadowing brim, Curly's expression didn't change, but his eyes were deadly cool.

"I'll handle Roderick," he said. "You stay at the ranch till I ride out. Now, go ahead."

Sheriff Nye waited until all the townspeople moved away from his office. Then he turned to Roderick and asked, "What in hell made you go down to Mex Town alone? You knew I was here."

"I didn't figure you'd come with me, Sheriff."

Nye fingered his mustache, thinking about that. The sound of footsteps behind him made him glance around, and he saw Judge Porter just coming up.

The judge was breathing hard from his run. "Is it true?" he asked Nye. "Did Duff try bushwhacking Roderick?"

"Yes."

Judge Porter noticed Roderick now. He stiffened. "That

fight," he said. "I should have known he'd be after you."

"He was after me for money, Judge." He repeated what Duff had said about the two hundred dollars.

The judge had raised one hand toward his fedora, but he stopped. He watched Roderick with a strained, listening look.

He said, "Did he say who sent him after you?"

"No. But I'd say it was the same person who had Stewart watching for me."

Judge Porter nodded, then sat down in a chair near the desk. He took off his hat and wiped his forehead.

Sheriff Nye crossed the small room to the gunrack and put the shotgun back in its place. He looked at Roderick. "What happened down there?"

Roderick told them rapidly, beginning with the boy's coming to Judge Porter's barn. Nye walked to the doorway and looked out, but listened carefully. The judge interrupted twice to ask who was at Tobrez's shack and what had been said. It was when Roderick mentioned the gun-running that Nye audibly turned from watching the street.

The judge said, "Did Tobrez have any proof of that?"

"No. But Maria Jack and Lerraza both saw the guns. And they heard Charlie and Haven arguing about gun-running."

Nye came back to the center of the room and stood there as though he didn't completely understand. Judge Porter had shifted his stare to the lawman.

"I went through the cantina after the fire," Nye said. "I didn't find any guns."

"Harry Stewart picked them up and brought them back to Wayne's warehouse," Roderick said. "There's no doubt in my mind that Wayne's connected to everything. Even the shooting tonight."

There was a small silence in the office.

Shortly Nye said, "Dan Wayne's down with a cold. He hasn't been in this town in the last three days."

"I don't claim Wayne did it himself. You saw Curly and Stewart in that crowd just now."

"Almost every man in the town was out there," said Nye.

"But only those two have been riding me since I got here," Roderick said. "And, damn it, you know they follow Wayne's orders."

Judge Porter cleared his throat. "Sergeant, if you had

some proof it would be one thing. But you have none. There's nothing connecting you to Wayne. Nothing at all."

"Look, Judge, my brother went to see Wayne that day. Wayne didn't mention that to me. Why would he hide it?"

When the judge did not speak, Roderick looked at the sheriff. "Did you know my brother and Haven were at Running W before the killing?"

"Yes. Dan Wayne told me Haven had trouble with Chico before over freight. Only it came to a head that day."

Roderick said patiently, "You going to let it go at that?"

"I'd be a damned fool to go after Wayne on just what them Mexicans said." Nye stood with his feet apart, thinking and still staring at Roderick. Finally, as if he'd decided what he'd been pondering, "Okay, finish your story."

"What about those guns?" asked Roderick.

"What about them?"

"There must be something you can do, Sheriff."

At that, Nye looked irritated. The expression was similar to the one that had confused Roderick when Nye had given him Charlie's belongings. Only it was more pronounced now. Roderick was going to add to what he'd said, but the judge spoke first.

"The sheriff is doing the only thing he can do, Sergeant," he said. "You know that."

"I know this is worth looking into, Judge."

"Damn it," said Sheriff Nye, "I am goin' to look into it. But, I'm not goin' off half-cocked. And, if there's any truth to it, it'll be handled right. Now, you got anythin' more to add to your story?"

Roderick breathed in deeply. Both these men, he knew, had to be cautious, but there was a lot of difference between caution and the way they straddled the high fence. Up till now, he'd depended too much on them. Now, Roderick decided, he had a right to apply pressure. And he knew where he would start.

He finished telling about the shooting, then went outside and along the boardwalk.

The sheriff returned to the doorway and stood there looking out, rubbing his chin as his eyes followed Roderick closely. In the long silence, Judge Porter put on his hat.

"Roderick's as honest as they come, Jaff," he said in a serious voice. "You don't have to watch him like that."

Nye merely nodded. "He's in it alone. He knows that now."

"That's the only way it can be, Jaff. He knows that, too."

Suddenly, Nye swore. He said with a bitter smile, "You know what I'd do, Judge, if I didn't have Alice and the kids."

Judge Porter nodded thoughtfully. "I'll have the will cleared in two or three days, Jaff," he said slowly. "He won't stay around long after that."

Nye didn't answer. He sucked in a deep breath, concentrated on watching Roderick.

Will Roderick walked directly to the Silver Dollar, and, as if casually glancing in while passing, looked through the top of the saloon's long, half-frosted windows. He surveyed each table, the bar, the man banging away at a melody on the tinny piano. Harry Stewart was the person he hunted, but he saw no sign of him.

Roderick stepped down from the walk and crossed Center toward the hotel. Even in the brightness of moonlight and stars, he noticed how he was being watched, but he ignored that now. No danger would come from people out in the open; he knew enough about enemy pressure to be sure now that anything shaping up against him would come as it had in Mexican Town, not right in the main street, with the sheriff watching his every move.

He went up the hotel steps and into the empty lobby. Sounds of movement came from the lighted kitchen in the rear of the building. Then Bainbridge appeared in the doorway. His fat face broke into a grin. "You ready to collect that steak now?" he asked.

Roderick crossed the lobby to the door. He said, "Which room does Harry Stewart have?"

"Twenty-three. But he ain't there." He moved his heavy-set body slowly back into the kitchen to let Roderick enter. "Harry rode outa town about ten minutes 'go."

"You know where he went?"

"Curly Gromm was outside waitin' for him. I figure he rode out to Runnin' W."

Roderick simply nodded.

"Well, sit down." Bainbridge gestured toward the table. He pulled open the icebox door and took out a long platter holding two huge steaks. Absently, he added, "Now Harry's gone, there'll be an empty place at the table for a while. More for the rest of us, anyway."

He chuckled at his own private humor as he slid the steaks into a huge frying pan.

"I'll have to pass that up," Roderick said. He thought of the long walk to the judge's barn. He might just as well hang out a sign telling his intentions as do that. He went on slowly, "You got a horse I can borrow?"

"You goin' after Harry?"

Roderick nodded again, waiting.

Bainbridge turned from the stove. He took two cups from a shelf, then lifted the coffee pot and began pouring. "If Wayne is out to get you," he said, "it could be he expects you'd start in on Harry sooner or later."

"If? Do you doubt it was me Harry was watching for?"

"No. I figured that all right. They figure you can hurt 'em in some way. So maybe they're watchin' for you to leave town."

"Who'll know, if you bring your horse around back for me?"

The fat man was thoughtful. Finally, he smiled. He took the pot back to the stove. "Here, you fix your own steak. You'll have time to finish eatin' before I get back."

He hesitated long enough to return his own steak to the platter, then left by the rear door. He went straight to the livery barn.

The long-faced hostler, his attention on stoking his pipe, showed surprise when Bainbridge asked for his horse.

"You ain't ridin' this time of night?" he said.

Bainbridge laughed good-naturedly.

"No, Ernie." His voice was casual. "But I'll be startin' for Ogallala before sunup. Figured I'd get everythin' set now, so I won't have to bother you so early."

"Well, sure thing," the hostler said. A few minutes later he brought Bainbridge's big black and white pinto from the barn.

After Bainbridge led the animal away through the rear alley, the hostler stood staring after him, still wondering. It was when he started into the barn that he saw Curly coming from the shadows on the far side of the work area.

Curly walked quickly. His face was completely blank.

"Why's Bainbridge takin' his mount?" he said.

"He's goin' to Ogallala 'fore sunup, and . . ."

"How often he done that before?" The eyes in the cowhand's calm face had narrowed.

"This is the first time. At least since I been workin' here."

Curly nodded. His narrowed eyes became hard slits.

"You tell nobody I asked, Ernie. Hear?"

"Sure . . . Sure, Curly."

The huge cowhand swung around and swaggered away, cutting down and soon disappearing into the shadows of the same alley Bainbridge had taken.

9

RODERICK rode northward at a steady pace, following the higher right bank of the Platte until crossing at the shallows about a mile below the Running W. Just before reaching the wagon-worn road that went into the yard, he pulled up to survey the ranch while the pinto blew. He frowned as he studied the slight outlines and surrounding terrain, for at night the sprawling buildings had a more concealed look than in daytime, with yellow lamplight illuminating only a few windows in the main house.

The moon, still hanging well clear of the horizon, would allow him little cover, the way it shone white on the flat. He sat there in his straight-backed cavalryman's way and looked around for the best direction of approach. He was intently conscious of the land now, even in the shadowy light, seeing how it was so wind-blown into sandy, dry washes, with patches of alkali and such spotty grass it wasn't even worthwhile for farming. His knowledge that cattle hadn't built this spread brought a strong regret that he'd not grabbed Harry Stewart out of the crowd at the jail and asked him questions then and there. But he held back his urge to hurry.

The chilly river breeze brought him snatches of noise; the whinny of a horse, a door slamming, the barking of a dog. Thy were all common ranch sounds, but in the quiet of the night and cool light of the moon they reminded him he couldn't be too cautious once he showed himself.

It was after more than four minutes' time that a door opened at the back of the house and a man moved into Roderick's vision. His body was etched vaguely against the light for only a fraction of a moment, making it impossible for Roderick to recognize him.

Roderick spoke softly to the pinto and turned onto the road. He dismounted before reaching the yard, so his horse would be downwind from the ranch animals. As he ground-tied the gelding, a light went on in the bunkhouse.

He approached the wooden building from the rear, then slid along close to a window and looked in. The short,

66

flat-faced cowhand named Forbes was sitting on a bunk halfway down the long, cluttered room. He was leaning backward, busy taking off his boots.

Carefully, Roderick turned the knob. Forbes looked up. An arrogant sneer came on his face when he recognized Roderick. His eyes shifted quickly to a holstered gun on the wall. He started to rise.

"Don't go for it," said Roderick. He noticed the holster was cut low, black with wear, and attached were straps to thong it to the thighs, everything branding Forbes as a gunfighter—two of them, Curly and this one, he thought fleetingly. His hand dropped to his side.

Forbes sat back. "What d'ya want?" he asked sullenly.

"Harry Stewart. Where is he?"

"He ain't here."

Roderick said, "He rode out here more than an hour ago. Is he up in the house?"

The short cowhand shrugged, not answering. When he again glanced at the gunbelt, Roderick said quietly, "Go ahead. Go for it, if you think it's worth it."

Forbes turned fast and looked at Roderick, his face still holding the arrogance, but now his deep-set brown eyes showed fear. He cocked his head then, as footsteps sounded outside. And he remained seated that way while Roderick moved back, behind the opening door.

Harry Stewart came sauntering in, letting the door slam behind him.

"Hold it right there, Harry," Roderick said.

The tall, bearded man swung around, frozen. His nervous eyes flinched uncomfortably. "What do you want here?" he said, talking hurriedly. "You ain't got no right comin' here."

"Get your stuff. We're going back to town."

Stewart looked at him with a puzzled frown. "Look, I didn't do nothin'. You figure I helped Duff take them shots at you?"

"Maybe. Get your stuff."

"You got nothin' on me . . ." His voice broke off. He gestured with both hands, a flush of stubborn anger coming into his face. His right hand began dropping down to his gunbelt.

"I ain't goin' . . ."

Roderick grabbed at Stewart so fast that the bearded man never got hold of the revolver handle. Roderick's right spun Stewart around, and his left reached down and came up with the gun. He threw the Colt behind the pot-bellied stove. Stewart began cursing.

"Cut it," Roderick said in a soft voice. "Quit the yell-ing." His right fist came up threateningly.

Stewart's silence was abrupt, an instant terror gripping him. He walked past Forbes and lifted his coat from a nail on the wall. He turned and stared hopelessly at Rod-erick.

"I tell you I don't know nothin'," he said. "You're wastin' your time . . ."

"Get moving. Pronto," Roderick said. He glanced at Forbes. The cowhand sat as before, not moving. When Stewart started for the door, Roderick took Forbes's gun-belt down and draped it over his left arm.

He said to Forbes, "Tell Wayne that Harry's going to talk to the sheriff. I'm not sure I didn't see him in Mex Town tonight."

Forbes nodded, still not moving.

Roderick nudged Stewart ahead of him. He pulled back the door and moved his arm out to push Stewart forward. It was then he saw the carbine pointed at him, even be-fore he heard a movement outside, or Curly Gromm's strained voice.

"Back inside," Curly ordered. He raised the Winchester's barrel a little, directly into Roderick's chest. And to Forbes he said, "Go get Mr. Wayne, Dave."

Forbes walked to where Roderick stood. He pulled his gunbelt from the outstretched arm roughly. He dropped it on his bunk and went out. When he'd closed the door behind him, Curly motioned for Roderick to sit down.

"He wanted to take me back to town," Harry Stewart said.

"You come all the way here for that?" Curly stared bluntly at Roderick, his eyes narrowed but controlled. "You got more to do than chase Harry here."

"Harry welcomed me to Buffalo. I feel close to him."

Curly grunted. "Don't try jokes. I don't like jokes."

"I didn't tell him nothin'," Stewart assured the tall cowhand.

"Okay, Harry, I know. I heard through the door."

Roderick said, "I heard Harry picked up some guns at my brother's cantina. He forgot to tell me about that. Or where he took them."

Curly's face didn't change. "Mr. Wayne owns the freight line," he said easily. "You ask him anythin' you wanna know about it. He'll put you straight."

"You tell jokes, too," Roderick said, his face hard.

A click sounded as the doorknob turned. When the door opened Dan Wayne walked in, followed by Forbes and a rangy, redheaded cowhand Roderick hadn't seen before. Wayne, gray-faced and gaunt in his loose-hanging clothing, gave nothing away. His expression showed only interest that Roderick was present. Curly lowered the carbine and moved around to the left of Roderick. Forbes halted on the other side and stood there watching like a wary dog.

"I thought you were going to ride out tomorrow," said Wayne. He spoke as though simply talking business. "Aren't you rushing things?"

Roderick said, "I came out after Harry."

"Harry? Why's he so important?"

"He picked up the guns Haven and my brother argued about. I thought he should tell the law where he took them."

"You were in a hurry, coming out tonight."

"I figured I could see the judge and get Harry under oath, so he can answer some questions."

"Under oath," Wayne repeated, considering the words. "You must think you have something."

"The judge'll probably want to know just how come both of you forgot to tell him about the guns. Or that Charlie was out here that day. Is that something?"

Wayne smiled faintly, but it didn't change the frown on his face.

"I didn't want my freight line connected to a murderer," he said. "Judge Porter'll see that."

Roderick looked directly into his eyes. "There was nothing more to it?"

"Can you prove there was?" Wayne's voice was cold and clipped.

"Duff might've had something to say about it."

"The blacksmith? Don't try tying up your personal grudges with me, Roderick."

Roderick looked at Stewart. "Whoever it was with Duff was tall and skinny. Harry . . ."

"Getting after Harry won't prove anything you've said."

"But Lerraza might help prove it," said Roderick.

Silence came then, stretching out while Wayne took a step backward. The quiet was broken only by clothing stirring and the men shifting their feet. A heavy warning rose in Roderick. He could die right here; he could sense it in Wayne's reflective manner and the cold watching sets of eyes.

"I heard Lerraza's in Mexico," Wayne said shortly.

"He is . . . for the time being."

Wayne smiled a bit grimly. "Your brother was out here with Haven. They had some trouble about a shipment of guns." He glanced at Stewart. "Harry did take the guns back to the warehouse. That's his job, driving for me."

Roderick remarked softly, "So, Mr. Wayne?"

Curly spoke up. "I'll shut his damn mouth. You let me handle him, Mr. Wayne." He was staring at Roderick furiously, ready to smash him with the butt of his Winchester.

"Quiet down now," Wayne said. The words fell demandingly, bringing instant silence. Wayne coughed, deep, chesty coughing. Then he added, "You go back to Buffalo, Roderick. Don't come out here again."

"What about Thompson?"

"Forbes told you enough. Tommy would only repeat what he said."

Roderick remained motionless.

"Git goin'," Curly Gromm snapped, pushing hard on Roderick's shoulder. "You heard what Mr. Wayne said."

The force of the shove made Roderick stand and take a step toward the door. He halted. "Okay," he said, looking about the room, letting his eyes touch Wayne and then Stewart. "I'll go. But I'll be asking Harry about those guns again."

"You do that," Wayne said.

It's a bluff, Roderick thought, watching Wayne, but he knew he was only fooling himself. Wayne wasn't one to bluff. He'd back up anything he had to. And right now he didn't feel he was being crowded that much.

Roderick made no answer. He turned and walked to the door, feeling the silence behind him, aware of the eyes on his back. And, he was also very much aware that his plan had failed.

He paused with his hand on the knob. For an instant he stood perfectly still, looking at Wayne. Then, he asked, "How are things going, now that my brother is dead?"

"What does that mean?" Wayne spoke carefully.

With his left hand Roderick opened the door. His right dropped to his side.

"I know about the gun-running," he said. "Charlie couldn't've been in on that alone. It was too big an operation."

He could feel the ominous quiet that rose in the room. Stewart watched Wayne worriedly. Roderick saw that, and how Curly had brought the Winchester up.

"Gun-running?" Wayne said. "I don't know what you're talking about."

"Those guns went somewhere," said Roderick calmly.

Wayne gave him a cold smile. "If I were you, I'd be careful of what I say. We have laws about slander. You might be the one to end up in jail."

Roderick stood motionless for several seconds, looking thoughtful. Then, without answering, he pulled back the door and went out.

Curly started for the door. The floorboards creaked under his quick step.

"Hold it, Curly," said Wayne.

"I'll git him. I'll git him, Mr. Wayne."

"Go after him here, you damn fool?" Wayne snorted. "Can't you see that's what he wants? This ranch isn't really connected to anything that's happened so far. We'll be playing right into his hands if there's trouble here."

Dan Wayne looked patiently at the door. When the sound of Roderick's boots slapping the stirrups came from outside, he turned again, but he did not speak until the pinto's hoofbeats had died out. His eyes were calm as he glanced at Forbes.

"Watch and see if he hangs around, Dave."

"Sure, boss." Forbes went out.

Wayne looked at Curly. "Why in hell did you send Harry out here?"

"I saw him come up from Mex Town, Mr. Wayne. There might've been someone else who saw him."

"What did you think it would look like, with Harry leaving town right after the shooting? Especially since he's been talking down Roderick all along."

Curly didn't answer.

"I gave you credit for more brains than that," Wayne went on coldly. He wiped a hand wearily over his forehead, his concern showing on his face, his pasty cheeks and jowls tight. "You do nothing on your own from now on. Nothing, you hear?"

"Yeah . . . Sure, Mr. Wayne."

Dan Wayne studied Curly blankly, but with speculation. "How about Maria? You talk to her?"

"She won't say nothin', Mr. Wayne." There was an edgy, charged quality to his tall frame as he looked down at the Winchester he held. "Only one who can hurt us is Roderick. Let me go after him?"

"And have Nye find him? Don't you think he'd figure Roderick was out here?"

"I could take the short cut and get back to town before him."

Wayne shook his head. He turned as the door opened. Forbes stepped over the threshold. "He's gone," he told Wayne.

Curly said, "He followin' the river?"

"Guess so. He don't know the short cut."

Curly looked at Wayne, his face pleading. "I can get back before Roderick. If I wait in town, they'll never connect it to us."

"Yeah," Harry Stewart put in. "He has to pass Mex Town goin' in by the river. It could look like a Mex did it."

"You let him talk to Ockers and the rest and even if he can't prove nothin' it'll make trouble," Curly said. "He might even come up with somethin' about Haven, Mr. Wayne. I'll make damn sure it looks like a Mex did it."

Forbes gestured at the redheaded cowhand and said, "Me an' Tommy'll go in, too. We'll make sure Curly don't miss." He took his gunbelt from his bunk and began buckling it on.

"Bout time we handled him." Harry Stewart glanced around, hunting for a rifle.

"Not you, Harry," Wayne said. "You stay here until morning. If Roderick's said anything to Nye, I don't want you anywhere near there."

"Then we're goin' after him?" Curly said.

Wayne nodded. "Just the three of you. Take him only if he goes in by Mex Town. He goes any other way, let him alone."

"Sure," Curly said. His fingers caressed the Winchester, and a faint cold smile twisted his lips. "Sure thing, Mr. Wayne."

10

T HE MOON was almost to the horizon, the river dark
and still as Roderick pulled the pinto in the cover
of some scrub willow and swung around in the saddle.
Despite the fireflies and humming mosquitoes that kept
after him, he sat for another minute without moving,
straining to catch any noise in his backtrail.

Shortly, he kneed the horse forward again. One thing
kept coming back to him: Wayne had his greatest worry
in Harry Stewart. This was something he should have
worked on immediately after the first talk at the Running
W. Now he realized his emotional drive to get his answers
too quickly had ruined his soldier-wise judgment. And, he
knew he'd not get another open chance at Stewart. Wayne
would see to that.

In the darkness he made slow time. The pinto became
impatient while passing the Mexican cemetery. He tugged
at his bit.

"Hold it, boy," Roderick told him softly, "you'll be home
soon."

The horse kept tugging, and Roderick reined in, sensing
something.

A faint metallic click reached him from the left of the
graveyard. An empty feeling of fear gripped him. Impulsively, he crouched in the saddle, dug his spurs into
the animal.

It came before he was fully prepared for it: a hard,
sharp smashing of noise from the left. Roderick felt the
shock of the bullet's impact at the side of his neck; the
power of the blow drove him into even more of a crouch,
the cutting pain forcing a hoarse shout from his lips. He
fought for his consciousness, held on for life.

Someone in the darkness shouted an order, his voice
loud. Two more rifles crashed simultaneously. The bullets zipped by overhead with the sound of cloth being
ripped. One ricocheted hollowly from a tree, making a
hateful, quavering noise.

73

There was no thought now but to get away, no effort at fighting the invisible enemy, no desire but to escape.

A gun flashed ahead, a second somewhere on the right. A bullet struck the pinto's side, thudding in like a hard slap. The horse slowed suddenly, jerked its head up and, whinnying in panic, began to stumble. With no time to swing clear, Roderick was thrown forward, slammed down violently, then sent sliding along the dusty ground.

He came to a rolling stop against some brush. His head began to throb, the pain growing until it slashed down his neck and along his left shoulder. Feebly he grabbed at the pain, felt the blood flowing. He lay there, pressing on the vein feeding the wound, panting for breath, trying to keep all sound down, for, not knowing who or how many were after him, his best weapon was concealment.

Five yards away the pinto had succeeded in standing again. It fled, whinnying in terror as it charged through the willows and splashed wildly into the river.

More hoofs sounded. A horse came along the edge of the flat noisily. In the vague light, Roderick recognized the approaching rider as Forbes.

"The river . . . he went for the river!" Forbes called to someone on his right.

Other muffled voices answered, unrecognizable. A second horse crashed through the brush nearby. Roderick pressed closer to the ground. The throbbing in his neck made him tremble. He gulped for air and fought the brackish taste of nausea flooding into his mouth.

From the river came a confused splashing of water, and shortly, quick conversation, accompanied by loud curses.

Roderick worked himself up to his hands and knees. One thing Indian fighting had taught him: in a battle, despite the danger, or wounds, you had a chance as long as you kept functioning. He began crawling toward the cemetery. Shouting and the sound of running came to him dimly from the Mexican section of the town.

He reached one arm up to the top of a large black gravestone and used it as leverage to pull himself to a sitting position. He drew his Colt and held it ready. In the distance townspeople were already going out onto the flat.

For long minutes Roderick sat still, while the hot throbbing subsided. He watched a few shadowy figures that had come to the river and now stood there talking. Forbes and the others who'd bushwhacked him would keep looking, then drift into the town and wait for him. He'd never make the sheriff's office or the hotel, he knew.

He sat there motionless for longer than half an hour. Gradually, the confusion on the flat quieted. Most of the townspeople returned to their homes. In Mexican Town the last of the lights that had gone on finally went out again.

Roderick studied the dark, irregular outlines of the shanties, and he thought of Tobrez. The little, scar-faced Mexican would do him no violence, even with the hate he felt. There was his only chance, he was certain. He decided on making a run.

He crawled past the graves. Beside the large cottonwood just outside the cemetery, he stopped to get his breath. He lay there stretched out flat. Finally he stood and, bent over, began to run. He crouched again, panting heavily while he rested near a pile of rubbish and boards and cans at the edge of the flat. He continued in this fashion and, groping his way, made progress between rests. When he reached the shed near Tobrez's shack, pain knifed his neck and shoulder and his breath came in ragged gasps.

He stumbled to the door and knocked gently. A grunt came from within. He knocked again. Bare feet shuffled on the dirt floor, stopped at the door. In Spanish, Tobrez said, "Who is it?"

"Roderick. Open up."

"Go away, señor. Go away."

"Open up. For God's sake, Tobrez, open up."

A lamp went on. In another moment the door swung back just enough for the Mexican's small, scarred face to look out. He started to speak, but stopped when Roderick pushed the door open and stumbled inside.

"Ai! Ai! You can't . . ." Tobrez swallowed his words and stared wide-eyed at Roderick's neck. "Mother of Heaven," he said.

Tobrez grabbed hold of Roderick's arm and led him past the table. He pushed the multicolored Sioux blanket to one side, then helped the wounded man onto a small bed near the wall. Gently, he began examining the wound, his stubby fingers feeling about with extreme care. The bullet had hit just above the collar bone, tearing a two-inch gash there. It was all caked over with dirt and dried blood.

"You should have the doctor," Tobrez said. "I will get him."

"No . . . no doctor."

"Señor, this is bad wound. It is filled with sand. I do not get doctor it will infect."

Roderick started to shake his head, and pain ripped through his neck. He lay back on the hard bed. "No doctor. You clean it best you can. Get the doc in the morning."

"But, señor . . ."

"I was bushwhacked, Tobrez. They're watchin' for me. You go after the doctor, they'll come here."

Tobrez straightened a bit. "It was one of my race? Ramon?"

"No. I saw only Forbes from Running W." He exhaled deeply and closed his eyes, letting exhaustion take hold of him. He heard the shuffling of feet again. He opened his eyes and saw that the little Mexican was gone.

Instantly, Roderick began to get up. Then he saw that Tobrez hadn't left the shack; he was kneeling in front of the corner fireplace, blowing on the flame he'd lit.

Roderick dropped back again. The sharp pain made him shudder. He lay quietly while the throbbing subsided. His eyes moved about the makeshift bedroom and came to rest on a large wooden image of the Virgin of Guadalupe in a wall niche. He was still studying the statue when Tobrez returned to the bed.

The small Mexican held out a tin can cut smoothly about the edges. "Coffee," he said. "There will be pain."

"Thank you, amigo."

Tobrez stood silent while Roderick drank. Then, he said, "You sure he was not Ramon? He has much hate, still."

"It was Forbes, all right." He explained what had happened at Running W and how he had been shot.

Tobrez listened, his face sober. He took a hunting knife from his trousers. "You roll over, señor," he said.

Roderick obeyed. Tobrez began cutting the bloody shirt where it had dried and become glued to the flesh. Roderick's body shivered as the cloth was drawn carefully away.

"There is much dirt, señor. It must hurt. I have nothing
. . . no brandy . . . no wine."

"You'll do your best, amigo."

Tobrez walked to the fireplace and got some steaming
water, then went to work on the wound. The probing and
rubbing were agonizing. Roderick clenched his teeth together hard, but nothing could control his shuddering.

For almost half an hour the Mexican cleansed the
wound. He worked slowly, taking much care with tender
hands and plenty of hot water, easing up when Roderick's body shivered, or the muscles in the wide shoulder
stiffened and stood out hard as wood against his restrain-
ing hand.

Finally he stopped and looked from the wound to Roderick's eyes. "I can get it no cleaner, señor. I should get
doctor."

"In the morning, amigo, when they can't hide in the
shadows."

"But there will be pus. All dirt is not out."

When Roderick did not answer, Tobrez went over the
tender skin for the last time. He tore a clean flour sack
into strips and bound the wound.

"You should sleep, señor."

Pain still lay in Roderick's neck, and his head throbbed.
His mouth was dry.

"Do you have more coffee?" he said.

"*Sí*." Tobrez went back to the fireplace and returned
with a steaming tin can.

"Thanks, amigo." Roderick drank slowly. He leaned
against the wall and let the hot liquid calm his insides.
After a few minutes, he said, "Did you know my brother
well?"

Tobrez shrugged. "No . . . not well."

"You went to the cantina, though?" And, seeing the
Mexican's nod, "What was Charlie like?"

"He had much money, señor. Much power. He was
good to my people. He was like one of us."

"There was no hate for him before the killing?"

"Not from my people. Many men in town didn't like
Chico for living with us. The hate from my people began
only after the murder, when it is learned about the gun-
running."

Roderick nodded drowsily. "How did you find Charlie?"

"He was friendly in his talk, as a young man is to one

older. But he was with the young men more. They knew him better."

"Did he have any business with Dan Wayne?"

"Señor, I do not know. Lerraza knew. And Maria. They were closest to him."

For a moment Roderick, thinking, was silent. The girl had not seen who'd beaten her. It could've been Curly, or Stewart. He wondered about that.

"Can you get Maria?"

"Now will be dangerous, señor," offered Tobrez.

"In the morning, then?"

"*Sí.*" Tobrez put a hand on Roderick's arm. "You sleep now, señor."

Roderick wanted to go on with more questions, but he could not put his thoughts into words. Exhausted, he lay back.

11

THE MOON had been down a good hour, but Dan Wayne got little satisfaction from that fact. He'd stood for the last twenty minutes on the porch of his house, gazing out at the plain. The stars glittering in the Nebraska sky threw enough light to give irregular silhouettes to every piece of timber clear to the flat. Once again he could picture the Mexican cemetery, with Curly and the others waiting there. It all didn't seem so foolproof now, even without the moon. And with the moon, there had been so much more light.

Roderick, he thought, might have been watching for a bushwhacker. That would account for no one's getting back yet. After the trouble inside the bunkhouse, Wayne would have been expecting a bushwhacker himself, and a sergeant in the army, simply from experience, would have been that cautious. He'd made a mistake in not having more respect for Roderick from the start.

Somewhere out in the darkness hoofs pounded on the dry flat. Wayne listened, judging the direction of the sound. Whoever it was approached from behind the house, not from Buffalo.

Turning on his heel, Wayne walked to the top of the steps. Then he stood still. Three, maybe more riders, from the hoofbeats. In another minute he could make out three moving forms. Across the yard a door opened and slammed hard. Footsteps shuffled on the sand. Harry Stewart's voice sounded loud to Wayne.

"Think it's them comin' back?"

"If it isn't, you remember they just rode into town for a drink," Wayne answered quickly. "We've got no idea there was a shooting."

"Yeah, sure."

Wayne's vision separated man from animal, recognized the lead rider's way of sitting his saddle. From that he knew it was Curly Gromm seconds before he could distinguish the cowhand clearly. Wayne felt relief, but still the impatience to know what had happened kept him cold inside.

The riders trotted their mounts toward the barn. Wayne could see Forbes and Thompson now. He called out, "Curly."

Curly's shadowy form drew up, then swung his horse across the yard. Behind him the others stopped. They moved their mounts at a quick walk to a spot opposite Wayne. All three sat more rigidly now.

"Well," said Wayne, "you going to wait all night?"

"I think we got him, Mr. Wayne," Curly began.

"You think? Don't you know?"

"We hit him, I'm damn sure of that." Curly continued to tell what had happened. He sat within three feet of Wayne, close enough for his bony figure to assume a definite shape. He couldn't be sure of Wayne's expression, but he knew the rancher's silence was just a mask to his anger.

"But you didn't find him?" Wayne asked sharply. "You didn't find anything certain."

"Only his horse. We followed him till he dropped in Feeney's south pasture. There was blood on the saddle. We know we hit Roderick."

"We kept ridin' round north," Forbes put in, "so we wouldn't lead anybody followin' back here. We didn't come in till we was damn sure no one was on our trail."

Silently Wayne studied the mounted men. His cold impatience had warmed to calm thought. Roderick could be dead, or he could've dropped off the horse anywhere between the cemetery and Feeney's. If the plan had gone wrong, the mistake was his own for depending so much on underlings who hired out only for the money.

Things had gone wrong before. Everything could have fallen through the day Haven came close to losing that shipment of guns meant for the Sioux. But nothing had been lost then. He'd taken his own action, had seen to it himself that it was straightened out. Now, if Roderick were still around, he'd go after him. He'd do it so all the town would be on his side, and he'd be right there when Roderick got his, so he could watch it happen.

"You all turn in," he said. "Be ready to ride into town in the morning."

The riders sat still, as though they expected their boss to continue.

Stewart spoke quickly, "I go in, too?"

"Yes," said Wayne. "We all go in."

Sleep came slowly for Roderick, with his dozing and waking at intervals. The pain died gradually, leaving only a throbbing that quickened if he moved. All during the night he was vaguely aware of Tobrez's presence, that the small Mexican's scarred face was close often when he was fed water or something else was done to make him comfortable.

When Roderick woke, the night had lightened beyond the window and was steadily giving way to day. He pushed himself up onto one elbow.

From the window, Tobrez said, "I send Tonio for Maria. She will stay with you while I get doctor."

Roderick sat up straight. He still felt weak. His neck and shoulder throbbed with a slow, steady rhythm. "Get the sheriff first," he said. "I want to get to the jail before I see the doc."

"But your wound will need cleaning, señor."

"Just get the sheriff," Roderick said. He rubbed his forehead, trying to ease the ache.

Without speaking, Tobrez poured some coffee into a can and brought it to him. "You rest, señor. I will get sheriff."

"Thanks, amigo," Roderick said. "God has put a good heart in you."

The little man remained silent.

Roderick reached into his pocket and took out the makings. He was lighting the cigarette when a knock sounded. Tobrez opened the door. Maria Jack came in. She spoke to Tobrez in a low voice, and, when he left, she walked to the table.

"You want coffee?" she asked.

"Just had some." He studied her with interest.

Maria looked away from his stare. One eye was still almost shut, but the swelling had gone down some and the bruise discoloring the left side of her face wasn't as dark as it had been in the lamplight. Her hair, heavy and black as a mustang's mane, hung loose, and against it, where her blouse was cut low, her shoulders were bronze and square.

She said, "I fix something to eat."

He shook his head. "I wasn't sure you'd come here."

"Tonio say Tobrez need me." She watched him, her expression not changing. She asked, "What do you want of me?"

Roderick leaned back, resting against the wall. It helped

relieve the hot thumping of the wound. "Don't you know?" he said.

"I think you have questions of Chico. You wish me to say he was not smuggling? Was that it?" Then, shaking her head, "I saw the guns, señor."

"Take it easy," Roderick said. "I know he got that shipment. But I hoped there might be something you remembered about that afternoon that could help me."

"There is nothing, señor."

"You heard the whole argument. And you're convinced Charlie was guilty?"

"Chico is dead, señor. It would do no good to . . ."

"Sure, sure," he said, cutting across her words impatiently. "He's dead, and for you it ends there."

"It is more than that."

Roderick eyed her silently. He snuffed out the cigarette, for smoking didn't relieve his soreness.

"You'll let it go?" he said coldly. "Let him be called a murderer? Let everyone remember him with only hate?"

"You do not understand, señor."

"I don't?"

"I sing in cantina for Chico, but it was more than that for me. You say all hated him. You are wrong. I did not hate Chico."

"You didn't speak. He was hung because of that."

"I could not have helped," she said in a low voice. "Nothing would stop the mob."

"Then you did hear something? Did that beating you took have anything to do with it?"

Maria glanced away, avoiding his eyes. "I know nothing, señor."

"Did Charlie deny anything?"

She shook her head. "I heard nothing . . . nothing that would help Chico. I . . ."

She stopped talking, for the door had swung open. Sheriff Nye came in, followed by Tobrez. Maria turned away from Roderick and looked down at the table.

The sheriff came directly to Roderick. "You shot bad?"

"I'm okay." Roderick looked at Maria. She did not move, nor did she lift her eyes. Roderick sat, aware of the soreness now, more than in his anger. "Maria hasn't told everything she knows," he snapped. "She's holding something back."

Nye turned to the girl. "What you say, Maria?"

"I know nothing of what he says."

The slim-shouldered lawman watched her for a few moments, frowning as he studied her bruised face. "That all you got to say, Maria?" he asked.

"I know nothing to tell, Sheriff."

"Damn it, there is something," Roderick said.

Nye watched the girl. He saw how pale and defiant she was, and that her lower lip trembled. He said to her, "You go ahead."

Maria left the shack. Roderick stared after her, a knowing look in his eyes. When Nye took Roderick's arm to help him stand, he said, "She was lyin', Sheriff. Anyone could see that."

"How were you going to make her talk . . . beat it out of her?" Again there was something hidden in the lawman's look, something grudging.

Roderick said hotly, "One thing about you, Nye. You don't push things, do you?"

"Not when it won't do no good."

"This time it would've, Sheriff."

Jaff Nye was silent, as though he conveniently hadn't heard. He pulled back the door and gestured for Roderick to follow him outside.

The sun rose higher in the sky east of Buffalo, yet for Dan Wayne the morning air still had not lost the night's chill. His bony figure, dressed in a tailored brown broadcloth and expensive Stetson, sat tall and straight as he turned his buggy onto Center Street and started past Mexican Town. He saw a thin column of smoke rising from Judge Porter's chimney. They'd be having breakfast. That was perfect, he felt, but that satisfaction did nothing to change his stern expression.

"Mr. Wayne . . . look down there!" Harry Stewart said, and Curly muttered, "So, that's where he went, damn him."

Wayne's brief glance between a row of shacks weighed what they saw. Roderick and the sheriff were coming toward the street.

"Look ahead," Wayne snapped. "Don't let them see you watching!"

The cowhands swung around in their saddles. Stewart looked at Wayne worriedly. "I didn't mean to . . ." he began.

"Shut up, Harry. Just shut up. And don't look back."
Stewart became silent, stared directly ahead.

Wayne shook the reins, making the horse move faster.
At the judge's front walk he pulled up. He pushed aside
the deerskin blanket covering his knees and, after handing
Forbes the lines, began getting down.

He hesitated on the step plate and looked at his riders.
Curly's long body was bent forward edgily. The others
were just as tense. Wayne liked that. When the right time
came, he would have only to give the word. They would
do the rest.

"Relax," Wayne said. "But if Roderick comes up here,
don't let him push you."

"He won't," Curly answered. He swung his big gray
around and sat silently as he watched Roderick and Nye
go into the doctor's house.

12

EIGHT or nine men were standing near the hotel porch. All were watching the doctor's house when Bainbridge stepped from the lobby.

"What's goin' on down there?" the hotel man asked.

"That Roderick," said one of the men. "That shootin' last night was for him."

"He get hit bad?"

"Couldn't be too bad. He can walk."

Bainbridge stretched his thick neck as he stared at Doc Merrill's front door. Three men were coming along the walk from that direction. One of them was Ockers, the dignified, well-dressed owner of the general store. Bainbridge called to the storekeeper before he reached the group.

"How bad was Roderick hit?"

Ockers glanced onto the porch. "Pretty deep neck wound. He's lost lots of blood." His voice was casual, indifferent somehow, but it silenced the small talk going on among the men.

"He say who did it?"

The storekeeper nodded. "The Mex are saying he claims it was Forbes." His gaze shifted, going directly to upper Buffalo and the cowhands from Running W. "That soldier's biting off a big piece if he goes dragging Dave Forbes into his trouble."

"Yeah," Hemeon, the gangling young clerk from the hardware store said, and he chuckled. "You figure Dan Wayne's askin' the judge to keep Roderick off little old Forbes?"

The chuckle was picked up by the listeners, and it bloomed into laughter.

"What's the matter with you men?" Bainbridge asked loudly. "You see anything funny about a bushwhackin'?"

The laughter died, was replaced by instant uneasiness. But no one answered. Most of the men still stared toward upper Buffalo. Those looking the other way watched Sheriff Nye come out of Dr. Merrill's office. Bainbridge

85

followed the lawman with his eyes, noticing how Nye paid
no attention to the people along the street as he headed
for the jail.

Hemeon's face had reddened. "Roderick ain't our worry," he said defensively.

"But bushwhackin' is," said Bainbridge. "Even if one
of Wayne's riders does it."

"There wasn't any proof of that," offered Ockers. "I
only said the Mexicans were spreading that story."

"Probably because it's Roderick's story," Bainbridge said.
"You think of that?"

The silence that followed lengthened until men began
moving off toward their places of business. Bainbridge
stood still, watching the turned backs. Suddenly he swore
impatiently, then crossed Center and went into the jail.
Nye was sitting at his roll-top desk. He glanced up when
the fat man spoke.

"Word's goin' around that Forbes bushwhacked Roderick," he said. "You goin' after him, Jaff?"

Nye shook his head. "Roderick didn't swear out a warrant."

"Hell, Jaff. You don't have to wait for any warrant."

"You know it'd do no good to go after Forbes," Nye
said in a quick voice. "Wayne'd have him out on bail in
five minutes."

"So?"

"So, if Roderick gets a warrant, I'll serve it. I'm bound
to do that. But I'm not bound to go tanglin' with Wayne
on my own. Anyway, the last thing Roderick wants is a
drawn-out trial. He'd be smart to let it slide."

"You're goin' to let it go, then," Bainbridge said sarcastically. "Just like when they lynched Chico?"

Nye's face became hard. "I brought Hopkins and Mc-
Cann in for that. And I fired Ayer. What more could I
do?"

Bainbridge held down his desire to throw the facts into
the lawman's face. He remembered the Jaff Nye of eight
years ago. He'd tamed the town with his guns. Buffalo had
grown so fast partly because of him. But that was before
Wayne controlled the ranchers in the county. The sheriff's
office wasn't an elective position, and Nye didn't have a
wife and kids then. Bainbridge understood all this, considered it before he answered.

"All right," he said quietly, "we can't help Chico. But

what happens to Roderick now he's got Wayne worried?"

"You really think he's got Wayne worried?"

For a few moments Bainbridge stared at the lawman. Then he shrugged off the inference and walked to the window. He pointed toward upper Buffalo.

"Have you ever seen Wayne ride in like that before?"

Nye stood and crossed the room. He did not answer, but stared at the group of town loungers who'd crowded around Wayne's buggy. They were doing a lot of talking to the Running W cowhands.

"Damned hangers-on," Nye said.

"There's more than one way of hangin' on," Bainbridge said, looking into the sheriff's eyes. "It all depends on where you're standin'. Don't do it, Jaff."

Nye, thoughtful and silent, still stared out the window. He saw Curly Gromm gesture toward Harry Stewart, call something to him. Then, Stewart dismounted and started up Judge Porter's walk.

"Well, Dan Wayne's gettin' the word on Forbes," Bainbridge said. "What you think?"

The sheriff's face was wrinkled, concerned, as if he'd been waiting for things to reach this point with fear and hopelessness.

"I don't know. I really don't know," he said.

Inside his office, Doctor Merrill was carefully cleaning the last of the dirt from Roderick's wound. The doctor was well along in years, a stringy old man with the juices of life dry in him, but his hands moved just as deftly as they had forty-odd years ago, when he'd started in the profession.

Now, he straightened up and stared down at Roderick over his steel-rimmed glasses. "You've lost a lot of blood," he said. "You should get some food into you. And some rest."

"I will, Doc."

A rustling of clothing sounded in the hallway. Roderick glanced up and started to his feet, but Doctor Merrill motioned him back. Just as a knock sounded, the old man asked, "Yes? Who is it?"

"Lucy Porter. I've got to see Sergeant Roderick."

The doctor hesitated. "He's not in much shape to see you, Lucy." He glanced questioningly at Roderick.

"Let me in, Doctor. I've got to see him."

Roderick nodded. The doctor opened the door. Lucy stepped hurriedly inside, but then she halted.

"I heard you were shot," she said. Her eyes were frantic as they stared at the ugly tear in his neck. "Does it hurt bad?"

"No. Doc here fixed me up good as new."

She stood with hands clenched, her clear eyes staring into his stubble-bearded face. She looked prettier than before, with her blonde hair soft and clean against the background of the sunlight from the window. She wore a pale blue dress that made her seem very young and feminine.

"Nothing to worry about," he said slowly. "I'm just getting a little extra rest."

Lucy nodded understandingly, as if she wished she could help.

"I know what you're planning," she said. "Please don't push things any further."

"I don't know what I'm planning myself, Lucy." Roderick's smile was oddly softened.

"You accused Forbes of shooting you. You can't go after him. Mr. Wayne'll have you hunted down. I heard him say that."

His face tightened. "You heard that?"

"He came to our house. He said you were at his ranch last night causing trouble over Harry Stewart. He asked Uncle to call you off before there was real trouble."

Roderick nodded. "I didn't know that Wayne and the judge were that close."

"They're not, really. Wayne was shouting at Uncle. He blamed him for sending for you. And he's going to speak to the members of the Town Council about it."

"And your uncle's on the spot?"

"It's not only that," she whispered. Her eyes filled with tears. "You have a right to be angry about being shot, and about your brother's death. But you can't fight Wayne alone. He's too powerful in this town. He's . . ."

"I know what he is, Lucy."

There was a silence, broken only by Roderick's easing out of his chair. As he stood slowly, he glanced at the doctor.

"You get me bandaged, Doc?"

Doctor Merrill nodded. He took a large bottle from a wall cabinet and opened it. The smell of carbolic acid sifted through the room.

Roderick went close to the girl, took her arm, and began moving toward the door.

"You'd better go now, Lucy," he said.

"You won't take any chances?" she asked.

"I'll be all right," he said quickly, intending to add more. But he stopped, surprised at how she affected him now that he was close to her. His pulse had quickened, and a warmth coursed through him. He kept his face from showing that. "Thanks for coming."

"I've never done anything like this before," she said. "But I had to come. I . . ."

"I understand, Lucy."

She smiled, more relaxed now. He stared at her soberly as she went along the hall. Then he returned to the chair and sat quietly, thinking while the doctor bandaged his neck.

Wayne didn't fear coming out in the open, but it was necessary for the rancher to make sure the whole town lined up with him, starting with Judge Porter. This was his main weapon: the people. They had lynched Charlie, and now Wayne planned to use them against him. Roderick smiled a bit grimly, thankful that Wayne, despite all his cleverness, knew so little about simple military tactics.

With that realization, Roderick's whole manner had changed. He knew he had the way to make the first crack in Wayne's armor, and that knowledge controlled his mind.

Dan Wayne climbed up onto the seat of his buggy. As he swung the vehicle around, he nodded for Forbes and Curly to pull in close. Wayne waited until they were well clear of the townsmen who'd crowded around the buggy before he spoke up.

"Where's Roderick now?" he asked finally.

"Still at Doc's," Curly told him.

Wayne nodded. He glanced at Forbes. "That talk can hurt you, Dave."

Forbes gave him a knowing look. "It worries me, boss. Maybe I should wait outside Doc's?"

"Mr. Wayne," Curly said, "I figured he was mine this time."

"No. Damn it, you do this my way." Wayne noticed that Curly had flushed at the sharp words, and he added, "You go after Roderick the town'll know I sent you after him.

But Dave has a reason. People will be expecting him to do something."

Curly stared ahead, saying nothing. Forbes glanced from side to side, his dark eyes judging the mood of those along the street.

"I go down to Doc's now?" he asked.

Wayne shook his head. "Let it build up. There's got to be no doubt about who people back up in this. It'll go all through town soon enough."

Nodding, Forbes straightened his stubby body in the saddle. Wayne felt the palms of his hands begin sweating from excitement. He held down any show of emotion, held down the urge he had to rush things. Time was on his side now. That time would allow him to get the town in just the frame of mind he wanted.

Roderick stepped from the doctor's house and walked up the street, squinting against the sun, hard and bright in the white dust. The town was still, with few people out, storekeepers opening up, railroaders and Mexican section workers going toward the roundhouse beyond the depot, and a few early shoppers.

Roderick slowed his pace to allow himself to pass two women crossing Center near the general store. When he went by them he nodded, raised his hat, then continued on, as if he didn't notice their questioning stares. In front of the hardware store he simply nodded to the gangling youth who was lowering the store's gray-and-white-striped awning. He didn't expect any sign of recognition, and got none.

He was almost to the hotel when he first saw the Running W cowhands. They were standing just inside the double doors of the Silver Dollar. Curly's face was shadowed under his wide-brimmed hat, but he was unmistakable. Forbes and Thompson were barely outlines in the saloon's dark interior. Roderick sensed the tension, felt it as one could feel the straining of a wire drawn too tight. He would make good use of it.

He gave them no attention as he went across the hotel porch and into the dark coolness of the lobby. He had taken only a few steps when he caught the blur of movement to his left. His hand snapped back and down to his Colt.

"I've been waiting to see you, Sergeant."

The quick words came from Judge Porter, standing behind the divan. Roderick let his hand drop all the way. "I heard Wayne was up to talk to you this morning, Judge," he said.

"Yes. He said you tried to take Harry Stewart from his ranch last night."

"I did." Roderick sat, welcoming a little time to rest. Now that he'd been on his feet a few minutes, he realized the wisdom in the doctor's words about food and rest. He felt weak, as though his strength were slowly draining out of him. "Stewart picked up those guns of Charlie's. I wanted to talk to him about it."

Judge Porter came around to the front of the divan. He took off his fedora and frowned at Roderick.

"Sergeant, I won't beat around the bush," he said. "That was a mistake last night. You . . ."

He hesitated when the front door opened. Bainbridge came in. The judge remained silent as the hotel man walked toward them, nodding to Roderick as he passed.

After Bainbridge was beyond hearing, the judge added, "I asked you not to start trouble. I warned you it would only make it harder on the Mexicans here. Now everything's beginning all over again."

"Judge, did you ever think about helping the Mexicans in a different way? Did you ever think of giving a good jail sentence to any man who gets after them?"

The judge did not speak. His face was stiff.

"Don't you see why Stewart kept after the Mexicans?" Roderick asked. "He was under orders from Wayne. As long as people here were kept busy hating them, they wouldn't get to figuring how Wayne was behind Charlie's lynching."

"Your brother murdered a man, Sergeant. He was killed because . . ."

"Because Wayne's cowhands worked up the mob so they'd have to lynch him. Remember, it was Forbes who brought the news to town?"

"Forbes had nothing to do with the lynching, Sergeant. His name wasn't mentioned at all in court."

Roderick thought about that. He felt into his pocket and took out the makings. Finally, he said, "What about my being shot last night?"

"Dan Wayne has five witnesses saying Forbes was at Running W last night."

"I saw Forbes out on the flat, just as clearly as I see you now."

"Then why haven't you preferred charges?"

"You said it yourself, Judge. Wayne has five witnesses."

The judge looked at him in silence for a few seconds, all the worry clear on his face. "So you're going to see it through. Well, I can't help you any more, Sergeant. I'll settle the will, and that'll be all." He put on his fedora. "If you stop by my office tomorrow morning, I'll have the final papers ready."

"Listen, Judge," Roderick said. "There's more to this than just the will. I don't know if Charlie was smuggling guns, but I do know there's gun-running been going on. Five out of ten of the Sioux have Henry or Winchester rifles. Some of the Indians I've run into this last patrol had Colts, too."

Judge Porter stared at him, an anxious look on his face.

"They didn't get all those guns at their trading posts, Judge. Sitting Bull's just waiting until he has enough armed warriors to go off the reservation again. Do you expect me to quit before I get the whole truth here?"

The judge didn't speak. He simply shook his head. Roderick wasn't sure if it was a reproachful action or if what he'd said had found deeper understanding.

He said, "Sergeant, you realize that if Wayne is hiding anything, there won't be a line he'll stop at now?"

Roderick stood, dropped the cigarette into a spittoon. His hand went to the bandage on his neck. "I figured he jumped that line last night," he said.

Judge Porter left then. Roderick walked directly to the desk. Bainbridge, sitting behind the counter, looked cool in his collarless white shirt with the sleeves rolled up. The hotel man made no movement at standing. Roderick saw why. There was a fine looking double-barreled sawed-off shotgun resting comfortably across his bulging lap.

This wasn't what Roderick wanted, for Bainbridge to get caught in the middle. He said, "You won't be needing that."

Bainbridge shook his head.

"Jim Feeney just told me he found my pinto dead on his land this mornin'," he said. "If I'd been sure what all the shootin' was about, I'd've tol' Nye last night."

"I'm sorry about your horse. I couldn't . . ."

A pudgy hand waved Roderick silent.

"Ain't just the horse. I saw Dan Wayne goin' from store to store just now. He's layin' down the law all over town. That's the kinda talk that starts a mob."

Roderick said bluntly, "You don't have to make this your fight."

"I know I don't," Bainbridge said. "But I can see what Wayne's buildin' up to, and I don't like it."

"What store is Wayne in now?"

"He went into Ockers's place."

Roderick nodded. "I'm going to take a walk down there. I want to see how far Wayne'll go in front of the people of this town."

Bainbridge stood. "I'll go along with you." He started to come out from behind the desk.

"Leave the rifle here," Roderick said.

"What? Them Runnin' W cowhands see you goin' in there, they'll come in after you."

Roderick said, "That's just what I'm figuring on."

He waited while the fat man returned the shotgun to its place beneath the counter. Then he led the way to the door.

13

OUTSIDE on the boardwalk the sun beat down on them. Roderick usually didn't feel the heat, but now, in his weakened condition, it seemed he sweated from every pore. His one glance across the street caught the blur of shadows watching him from inside the Silver Dollar. Roderick hesitated, as if he wanted to stay with Bainbridge's slower gait. In that same moment, he let his hand drop to his Colt and slid it up and down in the leather, then to his gunbelt, the gesture of adjusting his weapon automatic and businesslike.

He wasn't certain that the Running W cowhands had caught that movement. He wasn't certain that if they had they'd consider it a preliminary threat to their boss. He could only set the bait and play it through.

Roderick said nothing while they went along the walk to the next block, mounted the steps of the general store and entered. Before the screen door had shut behind them, he was staring back toward the saloon.

The three cowhands had come outside, Curly in the lead, and they were crossing Center fast. Roderick grinned, unstrapped his gunbelt as he glanced about the store.

Dan Wayne's tall figure, back to him, was near the center of a long, glass-fronted case. He was talking to the bald, prosperous-looking storekeeper. Neither had noticed him yet. The two women he'd passed on the street earlier stood out clearly against the background of bulging shelves and counters. And there was a young boy near the candy case.

Roderick decided on the position he'd take, clear of the customers. The gunbelt off now, he handed it to Bainbridge.

"What in hell you doin'?" said Bainbridge.

"Put it on. Don't come close to me."

"No, you'll . . ." Bainbridge's words failed him. Roderick had turned and was walking toward Wayne.

The storekeeper gazed toward the center of the room. He straightened suddenly. Wayne swung around and stared. A tense silence fell. The customers felt it and followed Roderick's movements.

Roderick went to the farther end of the glass-fronted case and stopped with the lower part of his body behind the counter. Through the window he saw that Curly and Forbes had just reached the porch. He leaned forward, resting his right arm on the glass. He nodded to Wayne.

The rancher, glaring, said something in a low voice to the shopkeeper. The merchant cleared his throat and swallowed.

"What do you want?" he said nervously.

"You're Mr. Ockers?" said Roderick.

"Yes."

"I'd like to put my horse in your livery. The hostler said to talk to you."

Ockers's hand shook. He glanced at Wayne.

"Roderick," said Wayne, "you were told you couldn't use the barn."

"I'm talking to Mr. Ockers, Wayne."

Wayne shook his head. "You're talking to me now."

"I'd like to use your livery, Mr. Ockers." Roderick's eyes were still on Wayne, but he knew the screen had swung open and Curly and Forbes had come in. He raised his voice. "What do you say, Mr. Ockers?"

"I've already said it for him," Wayne snapped.

The rancher noticed his cowhands then, saw Forbes and Curly, hands near their guns, coming toward him. Wayne's face relaxed. His look flicked beyond the two women and boy to where Thompson had halted beside Bainbridge. When his riders stopped near him, he nodded to them, his narrowed eyes ordering them to stay put.

"Get out of here, Roderick," snapped Wayne.

Roderick stared at Ockers. "I thought you owned this store."

"I do. I . . ."

Curly cut in. "Mr. Wayne told you to git, Roderick. Now, git."

That was what Roderick waited for, that and the frightened way the customers watched, even the gasp from one of the women. Roderick's glance moved to the right, past Curly to Forbes.

"You're a poor shot," he said.

"Not this close, I'm not," said Forbes.

"You were closer than this last night."

"I was at Runnin' W last night, soldier."

"A liar, too," Roderick said, smiling.

Forbes's eyes shifted to Wayne, as if asking a question. Roderick saw Wayne's grimace. He said, "Go ahead, wait for Wayne to tell you what to do."

"Don't push me," Forbes said, his face reddening.

"No danger pushing you. Not with the way you handle a gun."

Wayne spoke up. "I ought to let Dave loose on you," he said. "You'd better get out now, Roderick."

Roderick ignored him. He grinned at Forbes, who was flushed with rage. No sense in waiting, but he had to be careful with everything riding his next move. Wayne sensed what was coming. He took a step closer to Forbes. And in that motion, Roderick dropped his hand from the top of the glass case.

Forbes's gun-hand went down and back and came up with his Colt.

"Don't . . . don't," Wayne yelled. His bony arm reached out, hit Forbes's wrist violently. The sixgun, almost level, banged, spurted fire. The bullet crashed into the glass case six inches from Roderick's body.

Forbes, knocked off balance, caught his footing. "What in hell . . ."

Wayne snapped, "He isn't wearing a gun, damn you."

Roderick stepped out from behind the counter now. The relief he felt in tricking the cowhand did little to control the shakiness in his stomach. He was weaker now. His body cried for rest. As he started for the door, he heard Forbes's loud appeal, "I thought he was drawin', boss."

A noisy crowd was forming on the porch, a few men pushing the screen door in so they could see. Bainbridge, pasty-faced, stared with bulging eyes. The two women headed for the porch. The boy near the candy counter watched Wayne and those around him, listening, a bit dumbfounded at the confused talk.

When Roderick reached Bainbridge he saw the sheriff coming through the crowd, forcing men out of his way, pushing, elbowing to make better progress. Roderick halted and waited for Nye to get inside.

Nye shoved the last spectator from his path. He stopped just inside the doorway, his hand on his guns. His face froze as he stared from Roderick to Wayne.

"What happened?" he asked.

"Ask them," Roderick said, motioning behind him with his thumb.

Roderick knew that the sheriff saw he wore no gunbelt. As Nye continued into the room, Roderick pulled back the screen door. The spectators opened a way for him. One of the women customers was talking loudly, her voice, shrill and confused, carrying through the crowd.

"They were going to shoot him! He didn't have a gun, and they were going to shoot him!"

Roderick was aware of the eyes shifting to him, to his empty hips. Satisfaction ran through him. In an hour it would be all over town. It would be discussed, thought about. For now, that was all he wanted. He kept his face expressionless as he moved slowly off the porch.

At the edge of the boardwalk a hand tugged at his sleeve. He turned, began pulling away, but he stopped when he saw it was Lucy Porter.

"They shot at you," she said, breathless.

"I didn't get hit."

"Oh, I'm so glad!" Her eyes brimmed with tears, her relief clear on her pretty face.

The people at the edge of the porch had turned to watch. Aware of them, she dropped her hand. Roderick smiled at her. His face was constrained.

"You relax now," he said calmly.

She nodded, smiling. He continued on toward the hotel, Bainbridge following close behind.

Sheriff Jaff Nye listened carefully until Ockers told what had happened. Then he asked, "Want to prefer charges?"

The bald storekeeper glanced at Wayne.

"I don't know. I . . ."

Wayne broke in, "No sense in making a big thing of this." He gestured to where Forbes leaned against the dry-goods counter. "Dave thought Roderick was going for his gun, that's all."

"Somebody could've been killed," Nye remarked flatly. He nodded toward Forbes and said to Ockers, "You decide now?"

Ockers sucked in his breath. "I'll let it go, Jaff. I don't want trouble."

"You're sure?" And, when the storekeeper didn't answer, Nye looked at Wayne. "Would you say Roderick provoked Forbes into drawin'?"

"Provoked Dave? He could've meant to. But we'll let it go. None of us wants trouble with Roderick, Jaff."

Nye shrugged. "All right," he said. "We'll let it go."

"Jaff," Ockers said, "I don't want that soldier in here."

"He didn't do you no harm."

"I don't want a troublemaker in my place," the store-keeper said, his tone getting shrill. "I've got the right to keep troublemakers out of my own store."

Again Nye shrugged. Without answering, he turned and started from the store.

Dan Wayne stared at the lawman's back, tight lines forming at the edges of his mouth, around his hard eyes. Nye had seemed sullen, bitter, the way he kept after Ockers. It was a new attitude that Wayne hadn't seen before, something he didn't like at all.

"Mr. Wayne," Curly said, "we could talk up this trouble between Dave and Rod . . ."

"Damn it, shut up!"

The order brought immediate quiet. Wayne's gaze had shifted from the sheriff to Harry Stewart, who'd come through the door. The bearded man's face showed his habitual worry.

Stewart stopped beside Wayne. "Roderick's gone into the Shiloh, boss," he said.

"All right, Harry."

"You want me to, I could keep an eye on him from the lobby?"

Thoughtfully, Wayne shook his head, then asked, "Have you any freight for Al Hannah's spread in the warehouse?"

"No, nothin' come in for the Double M in a month."

Wayne frowned and looked at his watch. "Put shipping slips on a couple cases. Load them, and anything else you've got for the spread south of town."

"Boss, I don't usually hit that section till Friday."

"I said you'll do it today. Go ahead. Get the wagon loaded."

The tension drained from Roderick's body slowly, his tiredness and nerves refusing to let him relax completely. He ate the breakfast Bainbridge brought in, but he didn't sleep that morning. He waited, leaving the next move to Wayne.

He knew his first objective was to get himself back into condition to fight. By moving the bed against the hallway wall, he combined that aim with his effort at defense. He lay there quietly, resting and keeping wide awake so he could watch the door and window.

Whenever he heard movement in the alleyway outside, he sprawled flat on the floor, not taking the chances of someone's spraying the room through the wall or window. But no one came during those long hours. Roderick finally began to relax in the stifling heat of the room.

He got a razor and soap and towel from Bainbridge and, despite his wounds, did a hasty job of the difficult task of shaving. He had a lot of time for thinking, about his brother and the whole dirty mess of the gun-running, of how he'd unknowingly made things worse for Tobrez and the other Mexicans; and eventually his thoughts drifted to himself and Lucy Porter.

Roderick had no control over the way he'd been drawn to Lucy, but his experience and intellect told him that he had no business getting interested in any woman, or allowing any woman to get interested in him. Especially someone like Lucy. She was too young. Also, his life was not what she would fit into. His was the life of a soldier. There'd no doubt be other battles, and he might not keep the luck he'd had in the past.

Sheriff Nye sat inside his office most of the morning watching the Shiloh Hotel. He'd expected trouble to break out at any minute. But none came, so he went to the German's for his noon meal, ate that hurriedly, then returned to his watching and waiting.

It was close to three that afternoon when the shouting started in the street. Nye dashed out onto the walk, saw the rider who had caused the sudden commotion. Nye recognized the bent-over rider immediately: Bill Cagney, who ramrodded Al Hannah's Double H. He'd driven the animal hard and heavily, from the white dripping from his bit. Cagney's long body straightened back as he began to rein in strong a hundred yards from the jail.

Yelling men closed in on the slowing horse. While Nye pushed his way through the crowd, he could hear Cagney's excited talk. The cowhand was in his forties, his sun-drained face rough and leathery. His brown sombrero was pushed back onto the back of his head, and he waved one arm wildly.

"Thirty head, I tell you," he bellowed as though someone argued with him. "They got off with at least thirty head, maybe more."

Nye called out, "When did that happen?"

"Last night," Cagney answered. Because of the people in close and all the talk, the horse began to back, wheeling his stern and switching his tail. Cagney held him down. "Last night, Sheriff. We didn't find out until this noon, though. Al wants you to ride out now."

The horse began backing again. Nye reached out and grabbed the bridle. He shook his head. "I don't know about now . . ." he began.

"Al's got Prescott and some hands from his spread out with him, Jaff." The loud voice was shrilly insistent. "They'll meet us south of Wills' Crossing."

Again Nye shook his head. "I've got my hands full here, Bill. I . . ."

"There's rustling going on." Cagney jerked the horse's head up and started turning the animal, as though he meant to ride off. "Al needs you. He said for me to bring you back."

"Sure," one of the watching men yelled. "Your job's to git after them cows, Sheriff." More spectators picked up the call and repeated it.

Nye swallowed. His hands tightened into fists as his glance slid across the waiting faces.

"All right," he said finally. "I'll ride out with you, Bill."

Footsteps in the corridor drove Roderick into action. He slid off the bed and lay prone on the floor, Colt in hand. A knock sounded on the door.

"Who is it?" he asked.

Muffled, Bainbridge's voice said, "Sheriff's out here. He wants to talk with you."

Roderick crossed the room and unlocked the door. Sheriff Nye followed Bainbridge inside. The mustached lawman seemed smaller, skinnier, beside the rotund hotel man.

"How's the neck?" Nye asked.

"Coming along. A little rest'll fix me up."

Nye nodded. "That's a smart thing for you to do . . . stay right here and rest up for one or two days."

Roderick rubbed his chin. He was more amused than surprised. "You ordering me to stay inside, Sheriff?"

"No. But there's not far you can go in this town. Most

of the storekeepers came to my office and asked me to keep you out of their places."

"No signs?" Roderick said, smiling. "I thought people here just tacked up a sign and that settled everything."

"There's no joke to this," Nye said, too quickly. "People don't cotton to you forcin' gunfights inside stores. No one wants to take a chance on you."

"I didn't know there was a gunfight, Sheriff."

The lawman's short frame straightened. He turned slightly, as though to leave, but then he hesitated.

"Roderick," he said in a soft voice, "I'm ridin' out to the Double H, south of here. They had some beef rustled down there last night."

"I figure that's part of your job, Sheriff."

"It is. So why don't you stay inside till I get back. I'd say you'd be smart to do just that."

Bainbridge grunted. "What're you fallin' for, Jaff?" he said. "Goin' out after rustled beef right now?"

"Anythin' happens in this county, it's my job." Nye's tone had become hard, and now he wore that grudging expression. "Al Hannah's missin' beef, and I've got to check on it."

"You gotta jump or you'll lose his vote," Bainbridge snapped, his face reddening. "Damn it, Jaff, you were chasin' rustled beef the day . . ."

"You go ahead, Sheriff," Roderick said, cutting in loudly to drown out the hotel man's words. "You do what you see as your job."

For a long moment, Nye locked glances with Roderick. Then, without speaking, he left the room.

Bainbridge glanced at Roderick, confused. As the door closed, he swore and started after the sheriff.

"Let him go," Roderick said.

The fat man halted, one hand on the doorknob, and stared back at Roderick.

"What in hell . . . didn't anyone tell you Nye was out huntin' rustled beef the day your brother was lynched?"

Roderick nodded, unruffled. "Wayne's making the moves now. If I stop Nye, he won't play his hand."

Bainbridge drew in a deep breath. He let go the knob. Anger still kept his jowls flushed, made his voice tight. "I've got chicken cookin' up. Might help you sleep."

"Sure," Roderick said, grinning. "No sense in starving while I'm waiting."

From the porch of the general store, Dan Wayne watched Sheriff Nye leading his yellow gelding out of the livery. Nye checked the cinch, mounted, then glanced toward the porch. He seemed to be on the point of coming out of his way to speak to Wayne, but then he swung the horse around and rode past Mexican Town.

Until Nye was well out on the open flat, the tall, gaunt rancher remained motionless in the heavy afternoon heat that pressed against his face and chest and neck. When Wayne saw Curly Gromm crossing Center from the Silver Dollar, he stepped off the porch into the blinding sunshine.

"We'll walk down to the bank," he said when Curly reached the boardwalk.

Curly wiped his red, sweaty face with a sleeve as he fell in beside Wayne.

Without looking at the cowhand, Wayne said, "How are they taking Forbes's talk at the saloon?"

"Jest like you figured, Mr. Wayne. Ain't a man in town who ain't talkin' about that grudge." Because Wayne only nodded, Curly walked a few steps in silence. "Dave's ready to go after him now, if you give the word."

"He'll go when I'm ready. Getting Roderick isn't as simple as handling Chico."

"I can handle him myself," Curly snorted. "You call off Dave, I'll go over to the hotel right now."

Wayne glanced at Curly, judging him. He was getting tighter and tighter, like a coiled spring. Added waiting would make him more dangerous, more deadly once he was turned loose.

"No, Curly, we'll wait until tonight. That'll give people more time to talk about it. They'll be ready for what happens by then."

"Unless Roderick comes out before dark."

"If he does, nobody pushes him," Wayne snapped. And into the listening silence that followed, Wayne said, "Maria's as dangerous to us as Roderick. We get her too, and no one will ever dig up this trouble again."

Curly remained quiet. He slowed his footsteps now that they had reached the bank. Wayne stared in the direction of the Silver Dollar, glanced at his watch.

"Dave's got a good five hours yet," he said. "You make damn sure he doesn't drink too much."

Curly nodded, then headed back toward the saloon.

14

RODERICK was awakened by a banging that seemed close to his head. Instantly, his hand went under his pillow and came out with his Colt. The room was in complete darkness. Pushing himself up onto one elbow, he stared blankly toward the door, then sat up on the edge of the bed. His neck and shoulder were stiff, but all pain had gone from his wound.

The knocking sounded again, louder this time, and he heard Bainbridge's voice. "Roderick! Roderick! You in there?"

"Yeah . . . yeah." Roderick jammed the gun inside the top of his trousers and felt around on the table for the lamp and lighted it.

As he crossed to the door, he took out his watch. Eight-twenty. He'd slept for more than five hours.

He opened the door. He saw Bainbridge, and Maria Jack standing in the shadows behind the man's bulk.

"She came up to the back door," Bainbridge said. "She made me bring her in here."

"Sure . . . come in," Roderick said. When he stepped back to let her enter, he saw how her face was twisted in fear. "What's wrong, Maria?"

The Mexican girl stopped in the center of the room. She was breathing heavily. "Curly," was all she said as she gasped for breath.

Roderick took her arm and led her to a chair. When she sat he asked her what had happened.

"Curly came with others to Jalisca's. He tell me I must get out of town." She hesitated, catching her breath again. "They take me outside, but in dark I get away."

It might be a trap, Roderick thought, but then, looking at the ugly purplish bruises on her face, he felt ashamed. Despite his rest, he was too tense. It was something he had to control.

He glanced at Bainbridge. "Any chance someone followed her?"

"Tobrez was with her," the hotel man said. "He stayed outside to watch."

"*Si*. I go to Tobrez first," she said. "He take me to jail. Sheriff is not there. Benito was there, but he cannot help."

Roderick nodded and lifted the pitcher of water from the dresser. He poured a glassful. "Relax now, Maria."

She took a long drink. "When we saw only Benito in the jail, Tobrez thought of you. We thought you would help me."

Nothing showed on Roderick's face as he pulled the Colt from his trousers. He returned the gun to its holster, took his gunbelt from the top of the dresser, and buckled it around him.

When he again looked down at Maria she seemed steadier, but her face was still pale and confused. They stared at each other in the quiet. Finally, he said, "There's nothing I can do for you, Maria, unless you tell me all you know about Charlie and Wayne. I've told you that."

"Everything I know, I tell you."

He shook his head. "You have not, Maria. Let's have it. Everything."

She did not seem to hear. She glanced down at her fingers, loosening and tightening in her lap.

Roderick felt his temper slipping. He bent forward and, gripping her bronze shoulders, yanked her roughly to her feet.

"All right," he said coldly. "Get out." He pointed to the door. "Get out! Now!"

Terrified, Maria stared into his eyes. She jerked her arm away from him.

"No," she whispered, bringing her fingers to her mouth. The lamplight reflected sharply from her gold earrings. "You cannot send me out."

He began to unlock the door. "Either you tell me what you know, or get out in that lobby and wait for the sheriff to get back."

She shook her head, her eyes unbelieving. "Curly will kill me," she said softly. She backed away from the door.

"That's right." His voice was cold. "They'll kill you."

Maria slumped into a chair. Her body trembled. Roderick drew a slow, ragged breath and again turned the key in the lock. He crossed to her. "Everything, now," he said.

The girl started to rise suddenly, but he forced her back. She turned her head away from him.

"There are some of my race I would hurt if I tell," she

said, her voice begging for understanding. "There were some more who worked for Wayne."

"Who?"

"Jalisca . . . and Tobrez. They work in warehouse."

"Did they know about the gun-running?"

Again she shook her head. "But Curly say if there's trouble, he will say they did. I cannot do that to Tobrez, to Jalisca. When I was alone, it was Jalisca's family who took me in."

"Then you didn't keep quiet for my brother."

"No," she said, looking into his eyes. "You see why I cannot speak."

Roderick frowned and asked, "Was Charlie running guns?"

She did not answer.

"Was he, Maria?"

"I do not know. I honestly do not know, señor. I saw the guns. Chico had them. That is all I know . . ."

"You must know something else, or Wayne wouldn't keep after you. It was one of his men who beat you, wasn't it?"

"*Sí.* Curly, he beat me." She shuddered, tightening her fingers so that the knuckles stood out white. "He tell me not to talk to you or he kill me."

"Maria," he said quietly, "once we get Wayne, there'll be nothing more for you or your people to fear."

She shook her head. "Wayne is too powerful, señor."

His voice became harder. "We can get a U.S. marshal in here if we get proof of gun-running. And the judge will have to try Wayne. Now, what are you hiding?"

"In a moment," she whispered. "In a moment, señor."

He straightened and took his shirt from the iron bedpost. He put it on and buttoned it. He looked at her.

"You ready now, Maria?"

"*Sí.*" Her face was calm, composed. "When Chico was lynched, Wayne's wagon come for guns. Harry Stewart take them to livery barn. I see this."

Roderick watched her, waiting for her to continue. When she only stared at him, he said, "What else?"

"Nothing . . . Curly find me watching. Stewart and Ernie, the hostler, unload guns. Curly threaten me."

"There must've been more to it?"

Maria shook her head. "I swear, señor."

Slowly, Roderick began to smile. He'd never connected

the hostler to this, or Ockers. But they were the ones who first went against him. Both were weak links, so weak Wayne had to go out of his way to cover them.

"Did Charlie say anything to you about the guns?" he said. "Did he deny he was smuggling them?"

"He said nothing to me," she said. "He just ride out with Haven to . . ." She stopped talking as a low shuffling of feet came from the hallway. Her lips shaking, she rubbed the palm of her hand against her bruised cheek.

An insistent knock shook the door. Roderick's hand dropped to his gun.

From the hall someone called, "Señor Roderick! Open up, Señor Roderick." It was Tobrez.

When Roderick unlocked the door, the little scar-faced Mexican stepped inside quickly. "They follow Maria and me," he said. "They are in alley now."

"No," Maria sobbed, "no."

She swayed and Roderick caught her arm. He said, "How many of them did you see?"

"Only the man called Thompson, but there were others with him."

Maria stared at Roderick, her mouth open.

"Don't let them get me," she whispered. "They will kill me."

Roderick tightened his grip on the girl's arm. He looked at Bainbridge. "You got any rooms without windows?" he asked.

"No. Hell, you can't keep her here. They get in here, we're cornered."

Maria began to weep. She clung to Roderick's hand.

Tobrez said, "Señor, if we get to the jail, they will not come in there."

Roderick shook his head. "That's a wide street out there."

Maria's crying was almost hysterical. Tobrez took her shoulders. He spoke to her, trying to calm her.

Roderick watched her, his face hard. It was an old feeling, having to face an enemy, but he couldn't take one bit of action until the girl was safe. The jail was his only hope.

"Cover the lobby," he said to Bainbridge. "Keep them in the hall till I let you know it's safe."

He drew his gun and went into the hallway, then edged along the wall to a spot where he could survey the lobby.

He saw no movement, heard no sound but his own harsh breathing. He continued on to the back door, locked it, and then crossed the lobby.

Roderick pushed the front door open slowly and, pressing his back into the wall, looked outside. The street and porches and walks were deserted and quiet, as though everyone had closed himself inside to get away from a sudden storm.

He studied the shadows and yellow beams of lamplight falling to the street from windows, the sharp brightness thrown by the lamp in front of the Silver Dollar. He felt the cold loneliness of a hunted man as his eyes flickered over the irregular outlines of the buildings standing tall and black against the lesser darkness of night.

Footsteps sounded behind him. Bainbridge watched him from the divan, his sawed-off shotgun held in front of him. Tobrez and Maria waited near the desk.

"How is it?" Bainbridge asked.

"Too quiet. I don't like it."

"We've got to get out," Bainbridge said. "The whole town knows Forbes is after you. That's enough excuse for them to come in here."

Roderick nodded. He gestured for the others to follow him out onto the porch. He went to the top step and stood there in plain view, hoping to draw fire that might come before the others stepped outside.

Across the street in the Silver Dollar a man's head stuck out from between the batwings. Roderick faced him, saw he wasn't one of Wayne's men. Seeing who was standing on the hotel porch, the head withdrew in an instant, like a turtle pulling back into its shell.

Door hinges squeaked behind Roderick and a rustle of a dress was loud on the porch. Roderick stepped to one side, still watching the street.

"Keep close to me," he said to Maria.

The girl muttered something; she tried to smile, but when the shout came, her face froze.

"Roderick!"

It came from across the street, the tone of voice making the name sound like something foul.

In a single motion, Roderick shoved Maria out of the line of fire and whirled to face the solitary, stubby figure of Forbes, standing half-hidden under the glare of the lamp in front of the saloon.

15

FORBES'S gun came up, flashed.

Roderick had started moving to the left, off the porch, even before the first shot was fired. That movement saved him. The bullet ripped the sombrero from his head, seared through his hair as, crouched over, he jumped down to the street. Forbes's second shot whacked loudly into the timber supporting the porch.

Still crouching, his own gun in hand now, thrust out, Roderick squeezed the trigger once, and then again.

Forbes staggered, swayed, pitched forward. Behind him, flame lanced the blackness of the alleyway. There was a sudden thin shriek from Maria.

Roderick hugged the ground as the next shot from the alley zinged above his head. He fired blindly into the darkness, then ran forward. Another shot from the alley would hit home, he knew, but he meant to be fighting when he went down.

A thundering blast came from the porch, the explosion reverberating wildly as it splattered the corner boards of the Silver Dollar and tore into the alley. Roderick glanced around and saw Bainbridge methodically stuffing another No. 10 shell into his sawed-off shotgun. Tobrez was bent over something on the porch.

No gunfire came from the alleyway. Roderick was still moving, up from the street and across the walk. Running boots pounded far back in the darkness. He slid in close to the building, firing twice at a movement near the end of the alley. A gun belched flame back there. Roderick used his last shot and immediately sprang across to the adjoining building. Mixed with his own noises, he thought he had heard someone cry out, but now only a confused, quick shuffling of boots came from ahead.

He hesitated long enough to reload. Then he fired one bullet and recrossed the alley. When no shots were returned, he went forward cautiously. At the back entrance he halted to listen. He heard nothing, but he waited be-

fore rounding the corner and breaking from the deep
shadows into the moonlight.

Heavy footsteps thumped behind him, and Bainbridge,
puffing heavily, crowded in next to him.

Roderick edged around the corner. He saw no sign of
movement. No lights shone from the line of closed doors
in the rear of the buildings. Bainbridge was beside him
again, his shotgun held even with his bulging belly.

"I don't see nothin'," Bainbridge whispered. Glancing
at the closed doors, he added, "Hell, they could've gone in
any place back here."

Roderick did not answer. He went ahead and tried the
door of the saloon, and, finding that locked, moved to the
next building. That was locked, too. As he walked back to
Bainbridge, he felt his head. Forbes's bullets had run along
the side, leaving a slight skin burn. He holstered his Colt
slowly, frowning.

"See who it was?" Bainbridge said.

"No," Roderick answered soberly. "Thought sure I'd
winged him, though. I'm certain I did."

Bainbridge shook his head. "He got Maria with that first
shot. She's hit bad."

In the darkness, Roderick stared at the fat man. He
swung around on his heel and went quickly down the
alley. Bainbridge followed. They walked past the people
gathered at Forbes's body, across Center, and up into the
crowd on the hotel porch.

Roderick pushed his way through to the center, while
Bainbridge tried to move the spectators back. Hatless,
elderly Doctor Merrill's bald head was bent over Maria.
Roderick could see that she'd been hit in the face. Her
right cheek and eye were covered with blood. She was un-
conscious. From her breathing he knew she was very bad.

He wanted to be hopeful. "What's the doc think?" he
asked Tobrez.

The Mexican shook his head.

Roderick nodded solemnly, his eyes cold in his hard
face. Impatiently, he broke out of the onlookers and went
into the lobby. He ran through the kitchen and went directly to Ockers's livery.

Inside the stable the air was cool and heavy with pun-
gent barn odors. The horses moved restlessly about in their
stalls, possibly sensing the tension of Roderick as he walked
toward the lone lamp hanging from a beam in the back.

Once in the lighted area, Roderick halted.

"Ernie . . . Ernie, you here?" he called.

From the small room in the corner came the scuffing of feet. "Yeah . . . I'm comin'."

The hostler appeared then, one hand holding his pipe. His eyes showed surprise when he saw Roderick. He said uneasily, "What you want?"

"I was told Stewart brought my brother's guns here?"

"Guns?"

"The ones that were sent to him by Haven."

The hostler cocked his head to one side, as though he had difficulty hearing. He frowned.

"Look, soldier," he said, "I don't know nothin' about any guns."

"Maria Jack saw you unloading them."

Ernie rubbed the bowl of his pipe into the palm of his hand, nervous and uncertain. "She's a liar if she . . ."

Roderick's temper snapped. His fist lashed out into the hostler's face. Ernie was slammed back against a stall. A bevy of noises went up from the animals, hoofs pounding, snorting, neighing. Roderick grabbed the hostler's shirt front and yanked him close.

"What did you do with the guns?" Roderick asked softly.

Ernie's body shook, fear claiming him. His tongue licked the blood oozing from his split lip. Roderick shook him, and he raised both arms to ward off the next blow.

"What did you do with those guns?"

In a high, whining voice, the hostler answered, "I only work here. I had no part in any smugglin'."

"Those guns were brought here to you. Where are they?"

"I just had them here that day, till Curly come from the Runnin' W for them."

"Why'd they bring them here?"

The hostler bit his lip, watched Roderick carefully.

"Every time there was a shipment of guns to go to Wayne's ranch, Stewart dropped them off here."

"How often did shipments come in like that?"

"Three, four times a month."

"All to Wayne?"

"No. Sometimes for Mr. Ockers, sometimes for Gooddale at the Silver Dollar or other people in town. But Curly took them all to Runnin' W."

"Where'd they go from there?"

"I don't know. I never saw them again."

Roderick loosened his grip. Ernie took a deep breath and wiped a grimy hand over his mouth.

"Where'd the shipments come from?" Roderick asked.

"The Henry people . . . Winchester Repeatin' Arms in New Haven."

Now, Roderick was thoughtful. It was a bigger operation than he'd actually expected. A lot of planning had gone into the handling of the guns, very careful planning, with this barn an important part of it. Wayne had good reason to fear Maria's seeing where Charlie's shipment had gone. There would be records at the gun factories. Wayne couldn't bluff them down or settle them by bushwhacking.

"Don't you leave here, Ernie," Roderick snapped. "You do, you know I'll come after you."

Roderick swung around and started along the aisle. Ernie followed hurriedly behind him.

"You don't blame me for the smugglin', soldier," he said worriedly.

"You had a part in it."

"I did wrong hidin' the guns. You're right about that. Sure you are. But I had no part in the gun-runnin'. I got no money for it."

"We'll let the judge decide how much part you had in it," Roderick said.

They were almost to the door. Ernie grabbed Roderick's arm. Terror had replaced his worried look.

"Wayne'll send Curly after me," he said, staring out into the street. "Lemme go down to the jail with you."

"No," Roderick said impatiently. "Only Benito's there. I'll take you in after I see the judge."

"But . . ."

"But nothing. Wayne won't know you've talked. You'll be safer here than with only Benito at the jail."

"That's right," Ernie said. He let go Roderick's arm and stopped at the door. "I'm sorry about the guns. You don't think Sittin' Bull's got any of them guns, do you?"

"The Sioux have carbines," Roderick said. "And they know how to use them."

"I'm sorry . . . really sorry," Ernie told him. "I wouldn't have a part in anythin' like that."

Roderick stepped out into the work area, happy to be away from the hostler and his burden of guilt.

When the shooting started, Dan Wayne had come out with the others who'd been inside the Silver Dollar. Now he stood near the batwings, scowling as he watched the gawkers crowding around Forbes's body.

Roderick's deadly shooting had shocked him, causing a feeling of respectful fear to mix with the rancher's hate. Taking a chance on losing Forbes had been a mistake. When he'd started running guns, he'd hired Curly and Forbes after very careful looking, for they were the fastest guns he'd found. Curly was a shade faster than Forbes, but Roderick would be a handful even for him in the open.

Wayne buttoned his coat against the night chill. The batwings close by swung out, and Wayne turned to see Curly, sweating from running, step onto the porch. Curly saw the rancher right away. He halted close to him.

"Come inside, boss," he said. "You better hurry."

Wayne, still scowling, stared at his cowhand. "Take it easy. Settle down," he said. He pushed past the doors and walked toward the bar. When he again looked at Curly, he read the worry on his face.

Curly said, "Harry got hit. In his side. He's in the back room."

"How in hell did he get hit?" Wayne's voice was low and cold. "He was only keeping the back of the alley clear so you could get away."

"Roderick came after me too quick. He'd've got me if Harry didn't stay and shoot."

Dan Wayne nodded, then crossed the long room to the rear door. Opening it, he saw Harry Stewart sitting on an upturned beer keg. His bearded face was a sickly gray in the lamplight. When he got close to him, Wayne could see that his body trembled. Thompson had opened Stewart's shirt and was trying to stop the bleeding.

Stewart stared glassily at Wayne. "I got shot, boss," he said weakly. He'd spilled quite a lot of blood already. His shirt and the top of his jeans were soaked with it.

Wayne examined him coldly. "Can you walk?"

"I don't know."

The rancher gave a glance back at the door to the saloon. Talk had started up again there. He couldn't keep Stewart here.

"Curly . . . Tommy," he said. "You carry him. Get him over to my room at the boarding house."

The two cowhands lifted the wounded man, but at their first step Stewart began trembling worse, and making low chattering noises.

"Put me down. Down!" he whined. And, looking at Wayne, "It hurts, boss. Get Doc."

"I can't get Doc." He gestured to Curly and Thompson, and they continued moving slowly toward the rear door with their burden.

Stewart started moaning. "No . . . no," he pleaded. "Put me down!" He grabbed at his side, pressed against the wound.

Wayne spoke sharply. "All right. Put him down . . . here." He pointed to the beer keg. "Set him here."

Wayne was silent while Stewart was returned to his seat, bent over and still clutching at his side, his body shaking. Wayne wondered how everything could go so wrong. Roderick was alive and he'd lost Forbes. And until Stewart was fixed up, he dare not go on with anything. He had to move him, or there'd be too many questions.

Wayne said to Curly, "We'll let things quiet down outside. Then you go down to the livery and get my buggy. Pick up Forbes's body and start for the ranch. We'll meet you with Harry this side of Mex Town."

"How'm I gonna put Dave in?"

"Just lay him in the back seat. Tommy will bring his horse around when we meet you. We'll shift his body there. You just make sure people see you're taking him back to the ranch for burial."

"No . . . no," Stewart said. "I can't stand bein' moved. Get the . . ."

"Shut up," Wayne snapped. "It gets out this happened here in town, you'll be tied in with Maria's being shot." He paused briefly, and added, "When we get you to the ranch, we can tell the doc it happened there."

Stewart nodded and stared down at the wide shadow thrown by the circular bottom of the lantern.

Wayne said to Thompson, "Go inside and get a bottle of whisky."

In upper Buffalo men and women, and some children, too, had come out of the big houses. They stood together on lawns, or in the lamplight of the porches, watching the center of town, where the doctor was having Maria moved to his office.

Roderick noticed the prosperous-looking Ockers in a group directly opposite Judge Porter's house. He felt the storekeeper's attention shift to him as he passed. Ockers's look followed him while he went up the walk to where the judge and Mrs. Porter stood on their porch.

"Could I talk to you, Judge?" Roderick asked.

Mrs. Porter grimaced. "Surely it can wait until morning," she said. She glanced across the street, concerned at how her neighbors were watching.

"No, this can't wait."

The woman sat down stiffly. She gave Roderick a cold stare as her eyes slid across his bandaged neck. The judge took a step toward the door. He looked tired. His voice had a deep huskiness when he spoke.

"We'll talk in my office," he said. "Come right in, Sergeant."

He led the way into his den, then went behind his desk. The shaded lamp overhead threw shadows across the bulging shelves of handsomely bound volumes. The same shadows accented the concerned look on the judge's face. His standing there, quiet and serious, increased Roderick's confidence. Now that they had the way of getting the proof, it was only a matter of time.

"What is it, Sergeant?"

"I talked to Maria Jack before she was shot. I got a lead on the gun-running from her, and . . ."

"Maria's wounded badly. She might die."

Roderick nodded. "I've got another witness for court, Judge." Quickly, he covered what he'd learned from the hostler, ending with, "We can send for records of shipments from the Henry and Winchester people. Once we've got them, it'll be up to Wayne and the rest to try explaining where all those guns went."

Frowning, Judge Porter said, "Who was in on it?"

"We'll have proof on Wayne, Ockers and Gooddale. There'll be a record of that shipment Charlie got. If there were others, we'll dig them out, too."

The judge sat down slowly. He rubbed his chin as he gazed down at the polished mahogany of the desk. "The men you named are all important men in this town. They'll fight this."

"We've got a witness, Judge, and we'll have the papers. When I have Ernie safe in jail, I'll go get Wayne."

Silence descended in the small room. Judge Porter sat

rubbing his hand aimlessly over the desk top. After a minute, he looked up at Roderick.

"You'd better put off making accusations until you have more proof, Sergeant."

Roderick stared down at him. "That'll give them time to get away."

"Not one man who is guilty will get away. There's no reason why they should find out about this. Only you and I know. And Ernie."

"Judge, it'd take a month, maybe longer, to get those records. There's no . . ."

"Those men have families here, and good names. I can't allow anything to come out until I'm positive."

"Well, damn it, I'm positive now," Roderick said, his voice tight. "I'm going after Wayne right now."

Judge Porter stood. "You'll do nothing until you have the proof," he shouted. "Nothing, you hear! I don't doubt you'll end up getting Dan Wayne on this. If he's guilty, he'll answer to the court. But I won't take a chance on having one innocent person wrongly accused."

In the momentary quiet that followed, the judge stepped around to the front of the desk.

His voice quieter, he added, "We'll have Jaff Nye hold Ernie in protective custody. I'll send to the gun factories in the morning. Once I get those papers I'll have every guilty man arrested. But not until then will I . . ."

Interrupting, Roderick said, "All right . . . all right. I don't need it explained again. I'll go get Ernie over to the jail."

Judge Porter nodded and preceded Roderick to the door.

"Sergeant," he said, "tell Jaff Nye I want him to swear in two deputies. If this does get out, he'll need more protection for Ernie."

Roderick left the den. He walked through the parlor and into the hallway. Lucy Porter was waiting near the front door. When she saw Roderick, she came toward him, her face strained with worry.

"I heard about the gunfight," she said, blurting out the words. "They might try to get you again."

"Wayne can't try anything more tonight," he said quickly. "He lost his excuse when Forbes . . ."

She shook her head. "But, he's still in town. Mr. Harsbro next door saw him in the Silver Dollar." She caught his hand tightly. "We have a guest room. Uncle will let you stay here."

"No." His voice was firm.

As he spoke the front door swung back. He turned and saw Mrs. Porter standing on the threshold. The elderly woman's face was dumbfounded with the suddenness of shock.

In the quiet, Roderick glanced at Lucy, seeing the helpless look in her eyes as she let go his hand. Mrs. Porter said nothing. She went past them, through the parlor, and entered her husband's den.

"Judge Porter," she said in a high voice, "I want you to speak to that man."

He stared, confused. "That man?"

"That soldier. Lucy has completely lost her head over him."

The judge frowned, shook his head. "Alma, I have something very important to . . ."

"You go talk to him now," his wife shouted, losing control of herself. "Right now!"

"Alma . . ."

"Right now!"

Judge Porter's jaw began to quiver, and he stared into his wife's cold eyes. Defeated, he nodded, and opened the door.

Roderick was halfway to the street when he heard the front door open behind him. He looked and saw Judge Porter.

"Sergeant, I'd like to talk to you for a minute," the judge said calmly. He came down the steps.

Nodding, Roderick returned to the bottom of the porch.

"It's about Lucy," the judge said. "She's such an impressionable girl. Your being here seems so exciting to her, so adventurous. She's only nineteen, Sergeant."

A rustle of clothing sounded in the doorway. From the corner of his eyes, Roderick could see Mrs. Porter standing there listening.

"Yes, Judge," he said.

"I don't mean to insult you. But she's been paying too much attention to you. I think you understand."

Roderick didn't answer. He waited for the judge to continue.

Judge Porter said, "We don't want her hurt, Sergeant. You do understand?"

Roderick's nerves were taut. With so much happening, the judge was taking time for this.

"I haven't been chasing after her," he snapped. "I think the problem's all yours."

He glanced up at Mrs. Porter, letting his hard eyes rest on her face. Then he turned and headed for the street.

Judge Porter went back onto the porch. When he stepped into the hallway, he saw that Lucy had been standing behind his wife during the entire conversation.

"Lucy, I'm sorry," he said.

The girl choked up, and she put her hands to her face.

"You had no right." She began crying.

"Stop that," Mrs. Porter ordered. She took the girl's shoulder and shook her.

Lucy would not look up. "You had no right," she cried, her voice muffled. "No right to do that."

Mrs. Porter snapped, "He wasn't interested in you. You heard what he said. He as much as said you were chasing after him."

The girl looked at her aunt, her face unbelieving, but she made no reply.

The moon had come up now, and, though not full, it was still bright enough to flood Center with its mellow light. Roderick walked quickly, his glance raking the width of the street and back again, probing the thick shadows.

He studied the tall black silhouette of the courthouse as he passed. A sense of frustration about Lucy had added to his own tension. At the end of his talk on the stairs, he'd seen her standing behind her aunt. Her face had seemed so small and young. He felt sorry for her, the way she had to live under her aunt's thumb, and how, since he'd arrived, she'd reached out to him as a way of escape. Vaguely, he wished he could help Lucy, or at least talk it out with her.

His mind dropped all thought of Lucy when he first noticed the Mexicans gathered in front of the doctor's office. They stood close together while they waited, looking quiet and strained, and doing very little talking.

If Maria died, they would take her body to their section and bury her. They could do nothing more, he knew, but keep on, hoping the feeling against them would eventually die and they could build up their lives again.

When Roderick was halfway across the livery's work

area, he heard the heavy thump of running footsteps far behind him. He swung around fast and saw Bainbridge waddling from the crowd near the doctor's house. The man came to a puffing stop.

"Nye's comin' back," he panted. He motioned with one stubby arm toward Mexican Town.

"He was bound to get back some time," Roderick said, annoyed. He started on again.

"Wait for him," Bainbridge said. "With him along nobody'll try to stop you from bringin' Ernie in." He grabbed at Roderick's sleeve, held him back.

Roderick turned to face Bainbridge, and got a glimpse of the horse and rider coming along Center. Nye had banked around from Cross Street at a considerable angle. He'd pushed the bay hard for a good long time, and would have trouble stopping him. Roderick jerked his arm free as Nye went past. He watched the rider until he began to pull up hard in front of the jail.

"Give Jaff a chance," Bainbridge said. "There was a time he'd never have ridden out like he did."

Roderick held himself rigidly and glanced back at the Mexicans. "How's Maria?"

Bainbridge shrugged. "Doc's still workin' on her."

Roderick turned again and went into the barn. Bainbridge followed alongside. When Roderick reached the lighted area in the rear, he halted.

"Ernie . . . Ernie?" he called into the small room.

No sound came in the heavy silence.

"Mebbe he went over to the jail himself," Bainbridge offered.

"No. He's here, all right," Roderick said. He went into the small room and looked around. He returned to the light again. "Ernie," he called, "we're taking you to the sheriff's office."

In their stalls, the animals became restless. For a long minute Roderick stood motionless, staring into the deep shadows. A squeak of a board over his head told him what he wanted to know.

He walked to the ladder that led to the mow.

"Ernie," he called. "It's Roderick. I'll take you to the jail."

There was the sound of movement, near the big door through which hay was forked in and out of the mow. More boards creaked, and the long, frightened face of the hostler looked down at them. Roderick saw the gun in his hand.

"Come on down, Ernie," he said quietly.

The hostler said, "Wayne's buggy's here. He's still in town."

"Once we get you to the jail, you won't have to worry about Wayne any more."

The hostler made no move at coming down. "I can see the whole barn from up here. I stay here they won't get me."

"You'll be safer in the jail." Roderick put a hand on a rung of the ladder. "Come down now. Stop wasting time."

For a few moments the hostler was quiet. Finally, he climbed down the ladder, slowly and carefully. When he dropped off the bottom rung, he brought the old Navy Colt revolver up.

"I ain't givin' this up till I git to the jail," he said.

"You keep it," Roderick said. "Better get what you'll need . . ." He spoke no further when he heard a door hinge creak under the pressure of someone's hand.

The three men looked toward the door. It swung wide and the tall, lean shadow of a man stood silhouetted against the town lights.

"Ernie! Hey, Ernie! Git on out here!" Curly's rough words echoed through the barn.

The hostler began to shake. Roderick pulled him backward, deeper into the shadows.

"He's after me," Ernie said. "He'll . . ."

"Quiet," Roderick ordered. They could have seen him come inside, could be trying to draw him out, he knew. He edged Ernie further behind him and made a gesture at Bainbridge, telling him to stay where he was.

16

Curly called again, louder this time. "Ernie! You in here, Ernie?" When he still got no answer the huge cowhand pushed both doors open wide. Then he started down between the stalls.

Roderick stiffened, his hand on his gun, but he relaxed as Curly went into one of the stalls and came out with Wayne's horse. He worked alone in the darkness, hitching the animal to Wayne's buggy. After he finished, he mounted the vehicle and drove off through the work area, leaving the doors open behind him.

Roderick stepped from the shadows. The hostler followed, rubbing one bony hand over the barrel of the old gun, frightened and uncertain.

"Stay between us now," Roderick said. "We'll go straight to the jail."

Ernie nodded and closed in beside Roderick. They got as far as the doors. There the hostler stopped short.

"Curly's still waitin'," he said in a high voice.

"Hold it, then," said Roderick.

He saw the reason for the sudden halt. Curly had stopped the buggy just beyond the Silver Dollar. With the help of two or three men, he was putting Forbes's body into the vehicle.

Roderick pulled the left door closed. He stood just inside with the others, watching, until Curly drove the buggy past toward lower Buffalo. Then he nudged the hostler.

Ernie moved in between Roderick and Bainbridge. They started for the street. They were stepping up onto the walk when Roderick saw that Curly had again stopped the buggy near an alley at the edge of Mexican Town.

Some dark figures came out of the alley. Roderick made out two horses and a tall person leading them. Curly was lowering Forbes to the ground so the body could be shifted to one of the horses.

"Get Ernie over to the jail," Roderick said quickly to Bainbridge. "Tell Nye to get down here."

Roderick waited until Bainbridge and the hostler were across Center. He could feel the perspiration coming out all over him as he walked toward the buggy. Two other figures had stepped from the shadows. One of them seemed weighted down by the second.

Moving closer, he made sure what was going on. Curly was leaning from the seat, helping Dan Wayne get Harry into the buggy. A low, whining moan came from Stewart.

"You having trouble there?" Roderick said loudly.

Wayne spun around, his face clear in the moonlight. He showed surprise, but that look vanished instantly. Curly and Thompson were rigid with tenseness. From the seat, Stewart's low moan broke the ominous quiet.

"What do you want?" Wayne said.

Roderick took two steps closer, but he kept far enough off so he could watch them all.

"You taking Harry somewhere?"

"He cut himself on a bottle. Had too much to drink," Wayne said calmly. "We're taking him out to my ranch so he can sleep it off."

Roderick saw that Curly had straightened and moved clear of Stewart. His hand was close to his gun. He watched Curly as he said, "From the looks of Harry, I'd say he was worse off than just drunk."

"This is none of your concern," Wayne answered.

He coughed, then spat from tight lips as he glanced at Curly, warning him to let him handle this. His bony face suddenly became lined with deep shadows. Shouting and the sound of running on a boardwalk had caught his attention, and he looked back along Center. When he saw that Sheriff Nye was coming, he spun around, and, mounting the buggy, quickly disengaged the reins.

Roderick sensed the desperation of the rancher and moved directly opposite the seat. It was touchy, with at least two of the three armed. He said calmly, "Sheriff's calling to you, Mr. Wayne. I think he wants to talk to you."

Wayne threw a glance behind him to see if he could get away clear. His wrists rose slightly, to shake the reins.

Roderick's hand went down, touched his Colt. "Hold it right there, Wayne," he snapped.

The rancher became rigid. Curly's hand dropped, but Wayne's words made the cowhand hesitate.

"No . . . not here," Wayne ordered. He looked at Thompson, his lips tight. "Get mounted, Tommy," he said. "You take Dave on ahead."

"Sure, boss. Thompson climbed into the saddle and began riding off, leading the horse onto which he'd tied the dead man.

Sheriff Nye reached the buggy. He halted and stared from Roderick's gun to Wayne.

"You leavin' town, Dan?" said Nye.

The rancher nodded. He gestured toward Thompson, who had stopped the horses fifty feet away and now watched what was going on.

"I'm taking Forbes back to my ranch," he said. "If I can keep from having trouble with this soldier, Jaff."

Roderick said, "You'd better have a look at Stewart, Sheriff. There's something wrong with him."

"He's drunk," Wayne said quickly. "And he cut himself on a bottle. He can rest up at my place."

"Stewart's been shot," Roderick said. "You look at him, Sheriff." He brought his hand around to the front, clear of leather, leaving everything up to Nye.

All eyes were on the small lawman. The curious people who had followed him from the jail were crowding in, waiting to hear, and Nye was very much aware of them.

Wayne looked at the sheriff, his eyes menacing. "You come to my place, Jaff. You can check him after Doc Merrill gets through."

Nye ignored that. "No, I'll look at him now," he said.

He pulled himself up onto the step plate of the buggy and bent over Stewart, who stank of liquor. His coat was wet clear through, as though he'd spilled a bottle on himself. Nye ran his hand inside the wounded man's shirt. He felt the warm, sticky blood, and the deep slash below the ribs.

He said shortly, "You'd better drive him back to my office, Dan."

"He's going to my ranch," Wayne said. "We'll fix him up."

"That looks like a bullet wound."

Wayne swore. "Harry cut himself, I tell you."

Nye was aware of the talk breaking out in the crowd, but his eyes stayed on the rancher's face: "I want the doc to look at that wound. If he says it's a bottle cut, Harry'll go with you. If it's a gunshot, he'll have to do some explainin'."

Wayne stared ahead. One glance showed him that the crowd had the horses penned in. He glared at Nye.

"I'll take this to the judge," he said. "We'll see how far you can go legally, Sheriff."

"You do that," Nye said. "You make up your mind. You drive back to the jail, or I'll get up on that seat."

"Jaff," Wayne said, "you're a damn fool to do this."

The rancher motioned to Curly to dismount, and after he handed the reins to Nye, he began climbing down.

To Roderick, Nye said, "Get up here and hold Harry."

Roderick pulled himself up onto the seat. He sat beside Stewart and held him steady. Nye shook the reins, and the buggy moved forward slowly. The spectators noisily surged back to keep out of the way.

A loud voice called, "Sheriff, you think Harry shot Maria Jack?"

Jaff Nye remained silent. The buggy cleared the crowd and swung around to head back to the jail.

Wayne watched the vehicle depart, his eyes studying the onlookers, missing nothing. He looked at those close to him, but not one glanced away from his stare, telling the rancher all he had to know. He started through the crowd. No one gave way to him.

Curly went into action then, giving the closest man in front of him a smashing blow, sending him sprawling. Immediately, the spectators opened up to let Wayne through.

The tall cowhand walked beside Wayne toward where Thompson waited with the horses. Once beyond hearing of the crowd, he said, "Harry'll talk, boss. He'll tell every damn thing he knows."

Wayne nodded. He did not speak until they had reached Thompson. "Then, you two keep going with Forbes just as though you're leaving town. Leave him by the river and bring your rifles up to the judge's. I'll be waiting there for you."

"People'll be watchin' us," Curly said. "That'll take time."

"Damn it," Wayne snapped, "you just get back to the judge's damn fast. We've got to get Nye as well as Roderick now." His face was stone, his eyes slitted in thought, for he had his plan. "Can't you see that?"

"Sure . . . sure, Mr. Wayne," said Curly.

"Come in by the back door," Wayne said. "Make sure no one sees you."

"Okay, boss."

"Well, just don't stand there. Get going."

17

HARRY STEWART did not speak during the ride back to the jail, nor did he talk while Roderick and Nye carried him into the cell block and laid him on a bunk in the closest cubicle.

Roderick got a lantern from the office closet. He held it close while Nye opened Stewart's shirt. In a cell nearby the hostler's long face was pressed against the vertical bars, worriedly watching what was going on.

Nye was bone-tired. His back and legs ached from his long ride, and his arms felt like lead weights. He was suddenly aware that his hands moved too clumsily; he worked faster, wondering what Roderick was thinking. A law officer who rode out of town knowing trouble was coming deserved contempt, yet Roderick had shown none so far.

Sure, Nye thought, he'd made and accepted his own excuse this afternoon, but now, with Maria dying, it disgusted him. He felt around the wound and said, "That's no cut, Harry."

Stewart didn't answer. He was breathing heavily and kept his eyes closed.

"You were in that alley?" Nye said. "That's how you got shot? Right?"

"No. I was drinkin' too much . . . fell on a bottle."

"You figure you can fool Doc, Harry?"

The sheriff waited for an answer, but when it was clear that Stewart would not talk, he continued taking off the bearded man's shirt. Two minutes later Doctor Merrill came into the cell block. He stopped just inside the barred door and stared over his spectacles down at Stewart.

"This who shot Maria?" he asked.

"I figure he was in on it." Nye glanced up. "How is she?"

"Dead . . . What did you think, with her face shot up like that?" the elderly doctor said angrily. He put his black bag on the chair and took off his derby.

Nye cursed softly, and then he said to Stewart, "You

124

hear that? There's a murder charge against you now."
He bent lower, his face close to the beard. "Tell what you
know about the shootin'. The judge'll . . ."

"I don't know nothin'," Stewart said. He looked away
toward the wall.

Doctor Merrill took the lantern from Roderick's hand
and set it on the chair. He began examining the wound.
Shortly, he said, "Bullet did that." He ran his gnarled fin-
ger across Stewart's side. "Went in here. Came out back
here. Might've nicked a rib."

"Well, what do you say, Harry?" Nye questioned.

Stewart did not speak. His body trembled, and he took
a deep breath, gasping, for the doctor had begun to work
at the edge of the wound.

Nye whirled around and walked from the cell and along
the corridor. Roderick followed him into the office. The
dark-skinned Mexican jailor and Bainbridge turned from
the window as they entered.

Bainbridge said, "Word's goin' round that Maria's dead,
Jaff. There might be trouble comin'." He nodded toward
the street.

The lawman went to the door. He recollected how it
was when they had taken Stewart from the buggy. Only a
few townspeople had been about the walks and street, and
a sprinkling of farmers.

Now it was different. There were close to thirty men
and cowhands standing together beyond the walk, some
talking, but most looking confused and strained.

When Nye appeared in the doorway, a few of them
glanced his way. A young cowhand called out, "What's
Doc say, Jaff? Was that a bullet that hit Harry?"

The sheriff nodded.

"Whatcha gonna do about it?" a stocky, round-faced
rider said.

"Hold him for the judge. If Harry shot Maria, he'll
stand trial soon enough."

"Like hell," the stocky cowhand said. He pushed past
the others and stopped opposite Nye, his thumbs hooked
in his gunbelt. "Dan Wayne'll get him off some way. You
know that as well as me."

A low grumble of agreement broke out in the crowd.
But it died quickly, became silent as the men waited for
Nye's reply.

"Wayne doesn't control the jail," Nye said, "or the

court. I'll hold Harry for trial, and he'll damned well be tried."

"No reason for a trial," the cowhand said loudly. "Harry's done worse than them Mex who shot Haven, killin' a woman like that."

"Let the law handle it," someone called from the rear. "One lynchin's bad enough."

More voices joined in. Nye offered no argument and did not move from the doorway. The crowd was divided. Those businessmen who depended on big ranches like Running W wanted no part of trouble. There were others, though, settlers and cowhands who resented Wayne's power, men who'd be happy to have the rancher's power broken. Something else was present here, too. Nye sensed it first when he heard the names Chico and Haven and Wayne and Roderick muttered within the crowd.

They were connecting the first killing to what Stewart had done. Possibly they had some suspicion of their own guilt in the lynching of Chico. Possibly . . .

It could get out of hand fast, Nye knew. He didn't want trouble. He wasn't even sure trouble would come. But he'd done enough waiting these last few weeks. He'd let his concern for his job and family decide too may things for him.

Talking would do no good, not with even one of these men bent on action. Suddenly, Nye swung around and walked to the gunrack. He lifted two double-barreled shotguns from their place and handed one to Bainbridge, the other to Roderick. Then he took one for himself and crossed to the roll-top desk.

He opened a drawer and brought out a box of buckshot.

"Load up at the window," he said, "so they'll know I mean it."

Roderick checked the shotgun carefully and loaded both barrels. He said to Nye, "You think this will hold them?"

Nye's voice showed the strain now.

"We'll see," he said.

Dan Wayne was aware of the bell ringing inside the judge's house as he worked the crank, but the rancher's mind was more on the street behind him. He had decided the best spots to place Curly and Thompson. He had also reckoned on the moonlight, so bright on the sand. Anyone coming up the walk would stand out dark and clear. That was one of the certainties on which he staked his plan.

Within the house a door opened. Wayne listened for footsteps, waited.

Again everything ran through his mind. He could visualize the Harsbro kid coming back. The boy would leave Roderick and Nye at his own drive. The picture was plain, the two men continuing on together, right past Curly and Tommy. Wayne's sunken cheeks were stony, his mouth tight as he concentrated, leaving nothing to chance.

It would work, he knew. For his own part, there were no doubts. Roderick and Nye would naturally be cautious. But they both trusted the judge, and that was Wayne's ace. The judge could be talked into this; if not talked into it, then threatened, for, despite all his high-sounding principles, he placed a high value on his own neck. Wayne heard footsteps inside now, and he nodded to himself.

Judge Porter opened the door. "Dan," he said, surprised. "I thought you'd gone back to your ranch."

Wayne didn't answer. He went into the hallway, then directly to the parlor. Uneasy, Judge Porter shut the door behind him and walked to where Wayne had stopped near the sofa.

The rancher looked at him solemnly.

"Dave Forbes was killed in that gunfight tonight," he said.

"That's the sheriff's concern, Dan. Until it gets to court."

"That's right. But Nye's got Harry Stewart in the jail. You know as well as me that if he goes to work on Harry he'll tell everything he knows."

"We can talk about bail in the morning. It'll have to wait until then."

"The way Nye's acting now, he won't allow bail on this. He'll send Harry to the marshal in Ogallala before he agrees to bail."

The judge merely nodded.

"You'll have to do something," Wayne said, breaking the quiet.

"I'll do what I can. But if it can be proved those guns went to the Indians, the government will step in. And Roderick knows how to get the papers he needs."

Wayne stared at him strangely.

"I didn't tell them anything," the judge added, his

voice asking for understanding. "But they've got the proof, and it's my duty to work with them."

"Stop that damn stumping right now," Wayne snapped. "They'll never bring out that proof."

"I'm sorry, Dan. I was wrong to cover up for you and the others, but that doesn't change . . ."

Wayne cursed, silencing the judge. "We'll talk out your damn conscience some other time," he said. "Right now .I want you to send that kid next door down to the jail for Nye and Roderick. Tell them you've got all the proof you need."

"But I don't have proof."

"Tell them you've got a confession from me. Tell them anything. Only get them to come up here."

The judge said, "I'll go down to the jail with you if you want to talk with them." As he turned toward the hallway, the ring of the back doorbell sounded, but he forgot it when Wayne shouted at him demandingly.

"You get them up here. I want them coming along the street. Alone."

Judge Porter's heart dived down into his stomach. All the fear he'd been holding back swarmed over him. "No," he said. "I'll have no part in anything like that."

Wayne scowled. "We don't get them, they'll put a noose around all our necks. Including yours."

"Dan, you know I had no part in that smuggling. My only mistake was in hiding the truth after Frank Green told me what was going on."

"You damn fool," Wayne snapped. "You ridiculous damn fool. Do you think I'd come here like this if it was just the smuggling? You think back. Remember how Green died—how his shack burned? And how Haven was killed?"

"Chico killed Haven."

"Judge, Chico didn't even know about the guns that were shipped to him. Haven was supposed to get him after they left my ranch. But he was too fast for Haven."

The judge stared at him, the sudden shock of realization clear on his face.

"We had to force that lynching. What do you think, Judge, that Nye's being called out that day to check on rustled beef was just coincidence?"

"Good Lord. You can't connect me to that."

"Ockers, Gooddale, every one of us, will swear you were in on everything. We'll swear to . . ."

Wayne stopped talking when he heard the kitchen latch click. He looked toward the doorway.

Mrs. Porter came in, walking stiffly. Curly Gromm and Thompson entered the room behind her. Both cowhands carried Winchesters. They halted just inside the doorway.

"These men claim to have business with you, Judge Porter," she said glancing distastefully at the weapons.

"All right, Alma. I'll take care of this."

The woman started to leave. Dan Wayne had been watching his cowhands, but now he eyed her, considering her carefully.

"You stay here, Mrs. Porter." Then, seeing her hesitate, he spoke to the judge. "Well? You going to send for them?"

"I can't do that." The judge's voice was small and hoarse.

Wayne turned abruptly to the woman. "You knew that last year your husband was told about my freight line . . . that we were running guns and selling whisky to the Indians?"

Mrs. Porter drew herself up, stared at the rancher. "Yes, but the judge had nothing to do with that."

"He knew about it, and he did nothing," said Wayne.

The judge said, "There's no need to bring her in on this." He added to his wife, "You go ahead now, Alma. I'll straighten this out."

"There's only one way to straighten it out," Wayne told him with explosive fury. His patience vanished and he made his decision to go all the way; with Mrs. Porter in it, the judge would have to think of her too. "You send for Roderick and Nye, or we'll damn well drag your name in on everything."

Judge Porter shook his head. He glanced at his wife, read the sudden terrified disbelief in her face.

Wayne saw the woman's expression, too. "All you have to do is send the kid down to the jail," he said casually. He waved one arm at his cowhands. "We'll do the rest."

"No," the judge muttered. He swayed and put his hand on the back of the sofa for support. "Roderick and Nye . . . no, I can't do that."

"You can't do anything else." Wayne's voice was calm.

The judge turned toward his wife. His eyes swept past Curly and Thompson, and at that instant caught the movement of Lucy's green dress in the hall.

"Close the door," he said to Curly.

Mrs. Porter noticed Lucy then. Her mouth opened slightly, speechless, and a moment later she took a step toward the doorway.

"Don't leave," Wayne snapped.

Mrs. Porter stiffened, raising one hand to her mouth.

"I've got to talk to Lucy," she said almost in a whisper. "I've got to explain."

"No," Wayne said. "Get the girl in here, Curly."

When Curly swung around, Mrs. Porter pleaded, "Let me talk to her alone. I've got to explain."

Curly stopped and glanced at Wayne. The rancher was watching Judge Porter. He said, "You've got the girl to think of, too, Judge." Then, he added to Mrs. Porter, "Go ahead."

Mrs. Porter went to the doorway and Curly stepped back to let her pass. In the hall Lucy was staring at her, confused.

"You heard what was said?" Mrs. Porter asked Lucy.

"Yes." The girl regarded her aunt in stony silence. There was a disconsolate look in her eyes. "I don't understand how Uncle . . ."

"It wasn't only the judge," Mrs. Porter said. "When he was told of the gun-running, we talked it over. There were so many of our best families in it, he decided it was best not to bring it out."

"But the Indians got those guns?"

"You'll have to understand, dear," her aunt said. Voices came from the parlor, and she glanced back. Curly was watching them, listening. She spoke with quiet tenseness. "Your uncle will straighten this out. We'll explain it all to you later."

"Auntie, they want to kill Roderick and the sheriff."

"Judge Porter will never allow that, Lucy. He'll let them ruin his name first."

"Uncle should send down to the jail and warn Sergeant Roderick. He should . . ."

Mrs. Porter snapped. "That soldier. Will you stop thinking about that soldier?"

She waited for Lucy to answer, but the girl's silence insisted she go on.

Mrs. Porter added demandingly, "I'd think you'd forget that soldier and think of the judge." Her voice was slow, cold. "He said he wanted no part of you. You should loathe a man like that. Instead, you're putting him before your uncle."

Lucy's cheeks colored. She looked steadily back into the other woman's face.

The talk in the parlor had become louder. Mrs. Porter glanced worriedly that way. When she looked at Lucy again, her hand fluttered out impulsively towards the girl, but Lucy stepped away.

Mrs. Porter's face became frantic. She said quickly, "You let your uncle decide this. You hear?"

During the past five minutes, several more men had joined those already crowding the street opposite the sheriff's office. Their temper had changed, partly because of the stocky cowhand's haranguing, and partly because that was how a seething mob built up. They were talking a lot, arguing among themselves, but they were still all staying close together, getting angrier and pushing each other to the point where they could no longer be afraid of the law or the shotguns inside the office.

When a newcomer joined the crowd, the talk would increase, become louder, and eventually he'd either continue on down the street or, like the others, he'd take up the watch of the jail, his eyes narrowed by hate. Each man who stayed increased the possibility of their taking mob action, and more were staying all the time.

When Doctor Merrill came out of the cell block, Sheriff Nye shifted his attention from the street to the old man. "How is he?" Nye said.

Doctor Merrill didn't seem to hear. He was peering over his glasses at the street. He shook his head solemnly at what he saw.

"You plannin' to use them guns?" he asked.

"That's up to them," Nye told him, and he jerked his head back toward the cells. "Harry okay to talk to?"

"Sure he is. That wound ain't bad," the doctor said. "You'll have him in damn good shape when you hang him." He took a step toward the door.

Nye said quietly, "Doc, if you stay here you might help keep them men from makin' a mistake."

"This is your job, Jaff, not mine."

"I'd still like to have you stay, Doc. It'll help here."

The doctor's wrinkled face reddened. He gestured toward the cell block with one bony hand.

"I've given Harry all the help I care to," he said. "More than I think he deserves."

For another few moments he looked around angrily at all the men in the small room. Finally he turned and went out and along the walk past the window.

Nye kept silent, watching the street. He wheeled fast and walked into the cell block.

Roderick could hear the sheriff's voice, but it was so low he couldn't make out the words. A quick muttering by Stewart followed, then a shuffling of feet, and Nye's voice again, cursing loud and hard.

More and louder scuffling of boots sounded, and Stewart suddenly appeared in the doorway. His bearded face looked back at Nye, terrified as the lawman shoved hard on his shoulder. Stewart almost fell, but he grabbed at the iron-barred door for support.

Nye pointed at the street. "You look out there," he snapped. "They're waitin' out there, tryin' to decide if you're worth comin' in after."

Stewart swallowed and wet his lips with his tongue, but he did not answer. He looked down at the floor, paying no heed to the grumbling and cursing that had started outside.

"You'll tell me about that shootin'?" Nye said, his words distinct. "You want me to keep you here, you talk."

Still keeping his eyes down, Harry said, "I don't know about the shootin'."

Nye's open right hand came up and slapped Stewart's bearded face hard. Stewart's hands tightened on the iron bars.

The sheriff said, "Look at them, damn you. You look, and tell me about that shootin'."

Stewart stared outside again. "I didn't shoot Maria," he said quickly. "I didn't do it, Sheriff."

"You know who did?"

"No. I don't know." He bent to the left a little and held his side, still watching Nye, ready to duck his head if another slap was coming.

"You damn fool," Nye said. "You're keepin' shut for Wayne. Well, you see there out in the street? Is Wayne out there waitin' to help you?"

Stewart clutched at his side, wavering a little. "I ain't keepin' shut for nobody," he said.

Loud knocking sounded on the back door. Nye swung around, bringing the shotgun up, cocking both hammers in the quick action.

"Who is it?" As he spoke, he gestured with the gun, motioning Roderick close to the door.

From outside, a high-pitched voice answered, "Billy Harsbro. Judge Porter sent me, Sheriff."

Nye nodded to Roderick. "Just open it easy," he said.

He held the shotgun ready as Roderick unlocked and pulled back the door. The boy, blond and small for fifteen, was standing in the center of the doorway, blinking from the sudden light. When he noticed the muzzle aimed at him, he jerked his body rigid.

"The judge . . ." he blurted out. "He wants you at his house." Waving a hand at Roderick, "He's got papers or somethin' to show you both."

"Papers?" Nye said.

The boy stared at the shotgun. Nye dropped the muzzle down, and he added, "He say what kind of papers?"

"I only know it's important. Both of you, he wants."

Nye was thoughtful. He said to Roderick, "You go on up and see what he's got."

Roderick shook his head. "No, Jaff. You and Bainbridge can't handle this alone."

"Go up to the judge's," Nye said. "See what he wants. And ask him to come down here. Tell him I want him to talk to the cowhands out there. They'll listen to him."

"Jaff, this kid can get the judge."

"Don't waste time," Nye said. "Just get him down here."

Roderick saw that he could not argue with the lawman. "I'll have him down here damn fast," he said.

He gestured with his shotgun for Billy Harsbro to lead the way, then followed the boy out of the office.

18

BILLY HARSBRO hesitated at the first alleyway and pointed toward Center Street. He said, "By the street's quicker, but it's mobbed. I can take you around back of our house."

Roderick saw the crowded silhouettes of men standing on the walk. He nodded. "Okay. Go as fast as you can."

He trailed along, staying even with the boy. The moon was high now, so bright it was easy to dodge the brush and trees and fences, and even a shallow hole being dug for a cesspool in one of the yards. They had gone little more than eight hundred feet when Roderick realized he could barely hear the commotion at the jail.

He turned to look that way. His glance rested for a moment on the railroad tracks, glistening in the moonlight. The high redwood watertank beyond the depot stood like a silent sentinel, guarding the spacious plain that stretched to the horizon. Only the wind in the trees sounded along the peaceful landscape, the lack of sound accenting the irony of the night's stillness, masking the seething violence behind him. He tightened his grip on the shotgun and moved to keep up with the boy.

Staring ahead, Billy gave his whole concentration to his task. When he reached his yard, he spoke up. "You can cut through Ma's garden." He gestured toward the street. "Mrs. Porter said the judge'll be in the parlor waitin' for you."

Roderick gave the boy a quick nod. "Thanks," he said, and he continued on past the garden and into the judge's back yard.

He cut across the wide lawn to the drive. As he neared the kitchen he saw Mrs. Porter through the curtains. If he brought the judge back as he'd come, he realized, it would save all the time and effort of going through the crowded street. He went up the steps to the rear porch and knocked.

Mrs. Porter's face fell as she opened the door. She became breathless. "Judge Porter's in the parlor." Her voice was high and tense.

134

Roderick stared at her, puzzled. "Would you ask him to come out here? Sheriff wants him down at the jail."

"He's in the parlor," she said in a constrained, lower voice. "Go around on the lawn." She began shutting the door.

Before she had the door fully closed, she saw that Roderick had turned and was going down the steps.

Behind her, Lucy came in from the parlor.

"Who was that, Auntie?" she asked. The woman swung around fast. Lucy looked at her, baffled, and then started across the kitchen. "Who was that?" she repeated.

A frantic look froze on the wrinkled face. "Billy . . . Billy Harsbro," Mrs. Porter said. Her hand gripped the doorknob so tensely her knuckles had turned white. "His mother sent him over."

"Billy?" Lucy noticed the white-knuckled hand and the desperate stare. "Auntie, you didn't send Billy?" She yanked the hand away, then swung the door back.

Her voice echoed in the quiet of the night. She called out the name again as she dashed down the steps and onto the drive.

At that instant she heard a movement on the lawn, and she saw the tall dark outline of a man looking back at her from near the end of the front porch.

"Sergeant! Get down, Sergeant!" She began running to him. "Get down! Down!"

Roderick had stopped walking when he'd heard Lucy's first yell for the Harsbro boy. Now, with the shouted warning, he was in motion, throwing himself backward, headlong for the drive.

Across the street a rifle banged. The bullet zinged above him. Another bullet followed immediately, and it whacked like a lightning crack into the side of the house.

Hatless, Roderick sprawled awkwardly, watching for a gunflash. Lucy, her body bent over almost double, slid in close to him and flattened out.

"Oh, Lord," she said. "Lord!" She breathed heavily, panted for air.

"You knew they were there? You knew, Lucy?"

"Yes . . . yes. Mr. Wayne's got Thompson right across the street. Curly's on the next lawn, in Ockers's cotton-woods. I didn't know Auntie sent for you. I didn't know."

"Two of them? Only two? Where's Wayne?"

"In the house." She still panted, but her breath came more easily. "He threatened Uncle if he didn't set you and the sheriff up for him. Auntie thought she was helping . . ."

Roderick said quickly, "You sure only Thompson and Curly are over there?"

"Yes . . . they're right where I told you."

A shiver of excitement went down Roderick's spine as he pushed himself up to study the street, clear and white in the floodlight moon. He calmed, surveyed the terrain. The distance was too long for a belt-gun.

"Just lie flat and you'll be safe," he said.

She grabbed his arm. "Stay here. They'll be coming up from the jail. The sheriff'll be . . ."

"Nye got his own hands full." Roderick started to move away toward the large cottonwood at the end of the drive. But she began to follow and he hesitated. "Stay here under cover," he ordered.

Then, seeing she was again motionless, he continued crawling. When he reached the cover of the cottonwood, he peered around the trunk, listened for sound of movement across the street. From behind him came the rustle of a dress and the crunch of footsteps on sand. Lucy stumbled in beside him.

"I told you to stay put," he said.

"No. I can help."

"Get back there."

"No."

He glanced angrily at her. He stared into a face as stubborn as his own.

Waiting for him to speak, she pressed close to him, so close he could feel her trembling. And he'd only rebuffed this girl all along, he thought fleetingly. How wrong he had been. He wanted to reach out and put his arm around her, to hold her close. He drove the impulse from his mind.

"Can you handle a shotgun, Lucy?"

"Yes."

He held out the weapon. "Stay behind this tree. When I give the word, you fire toward Thompson," he ordered.

She said frantically, "We should wait for the sheriff."

"Nye's got a mob to hold down at the jail," Roderick told her. He stared across the street, said finally, "Okay . . . draw Thompson's fire."

The girl squeezed one trigger. The shotgun thundered.

Directly across the street flame lanced the darkness of a deep shadow, the explosion of Thompson's carbine blending with the shotgun's echo. Roderick shot four times in rapid succession at the spot where he'd seen the lancing flame.

A muffled cry came from Thompson. Twenty yards away on the same side another carbine cracked from among a clustered shadow that outlined the trees on Ockers's lawn.

Lucy would be safe, he knew, as long as she kept behind the tree. He dug into his pocket and took out the extra shells Nye had given him. He passed them to her.

"Okay, reload," he said.

As the girl reloaded, Roderick filled the empty chambers of his sixgun. Lights had gone on all along the street, and not too far away a window was being opened.

"Listen now," Roderick said. "Fire once into the air. I'll get across the street in the gunflash."

"He'll see you."

"Not if I move with the flash," he said. "You stay under cover here. Give me half a minute, then fire over those trees Curly's in. Over the trees. I want him alive."

Lucy did not answer. Roderick saw her aim. He was moving fast as the shotgun belched flame again, and he made it across the street. From the cottonwoods Curly returned the fire as fast as he could pump his rifle.

Roderick found Thompson where he'd dropped. He halted at the body and turned it with his boot. Thompson rolled over and lay still. Roderick went into action again at Lucy's next shot, moving up close to Ockers's porch, utilizing the shadows there and any sound to cover his own.

Curly kept pounding away at the shotgun flashes. Roderick had the advantage he needed now, enabling him to go after his enemy on his own terms.

After another blast from the shotgun, Roderick reached the edge of the trees on the long lawn. He had Curly spotted clearly from the flashes of the carbine.

He got close enough to make out Curly's bulky form before the cowhand stopped firing.

Curly was reloading, his long face blanked out by the brim of his sombrero. Roderick raced forward, beginning his charge as closely as possible, his Colt poised for a blow. When he was five yards from Curly, the cowhand looked up.

"Tommy . . . that you, Tom . . ." Instinctively, Curly swung out with the Winchester, and the weapon's stock bounced off Roderick's side.

Curly ducked to the left, trying to protect his face. He drew the rifle back for another blow.

But Roderick was on him, slamming the Colt down on the big head. He felt the shock of the barrel's impact jolt his arm. Curly grunted and staggered back, one outstretched hand grabbing for Roderick's pounding shoulder.

Roderick followed him down, caught in the powerful grip. Savagely, he drove the gun down once, and again, and again, lost in the violence of his anger. He felt the warm blood flowing along his neck, where his wound had reopened. He smashed at Curly's face. Then Curly's grip broke, and the cowhand dropped backward.

Roderick kicked the Winchester away from Curly's reach. Gasping for air, he leveled the Colt, straightened and waited.

Curly moaned, grunted, and began getting to his feet.

"One step," Roderick said, "and I'll kill you."

For a few seconds, Curly, still dazed, just glared at Roderick. He spat blood from his shattered mouth. Finally, his right hand began to drop.

"Go ahead," Roderick said. "That's just what I want. Go ahead."

Curly froze, then raised his arms above his head.

Roughly, Roderick swung him around and yanked his gun from its holster. "Get walking," he ordered.

Curly began moving forward.

Roderick called out, "Don't shoot, Lucy. We're crossing over now. Don't shoot!"

When Judge Porter heard Roderick's words, he ran down the drive toward the cottonwood tree.

"Lucy, are you all right?" he called. "Lucy!"

"Yes." She stepped from the darkness of the tree.

The judge stopped beside her. "We didn't know what happened to you," he said as he took the shotgun from her. She didn't answer. She had been watching the shadowy figures of the two men coming across the street, but now she noticed Dan Wayne had stepped out onto the porch. Wayne stood, tall and gaunt and stoop-shouldered, with one hand behind him. Lucy could see the stubby derringer Wayne held in that hand.

"No!" she shouted. "No!"

Judge Porter heard her cry, saw the derringer too. He started for the porch, but went only a few feet before he stopped.

Wayne had waited patiently until Roderick got close to the front walk. Now, his hand came out from behind his back, bringing the derringer up to aim.

"You'll ruin no more lives," the judge said quietly.

He pulled both triggers at once, blasting the rancher off the porch.

Sheriff Nye stared toward upper Buffalo from the doorway of his office. The gunfire had stopped up there, had been over for longer than a minute now, but he wasn't quite certain what that meant.

Behind him, Bainbridge asked softly, "Figure someone got Roderick?"

"I don't know."

"We could look?"

"No. We'll wait and find out what happens," Nye said soberly.

Nye studied the street. The gunfire had made the crowd more excited, scared some of them so they'd spread out more and formed a solid line that bellied out clear to the walk on the other side. Almost anything could come from a scared mob, he knew.

It could come now, unless he took some action himself. Nye did not look back as he spoke.

"Bainbridge," he said, "lock the door after I go out. Don't open it till I come back."

"You're not goin' up there, Jaff?"

"Lock it. Understand?"

The sheriff stepped onto the boardwalk. He heard the door shut behind him, then the snap of the lock. Looking directly at the men closest to him, he pointed to the opposite side of Center and said, "Get back over there."

When the cowhands only stared arrogantly at him, he swung out suddenly with his shotgun, bringing the barrels around brutally against the head of the nearest man, knocking him down.

"Back—over there!" he ordered. He shoved aside a

man who bent to help the unfortunate cowhand. "Leave him there. Leave him! Get back!"

"What in hell's wrong with you!" someone yelled. And a second voice rose up. "What you want, time to ride outa town, Sheriff?" Cursing, others joined in, but, reluctantly, those in front began edging back.

Nye didn't answer. He still held the stubby barrels pointed threateningly. He heard the quick, rising muttering grow louder at the rear of the crowd. The mutter and movement had caught the attention of those in close to him, too, causing them to look around.

People began opening a way in the middle of the street. Curly appeared first coming through the crowd. Roderick and Judge Porter were directly behind him.

Curly walked hurriedly, stumbling. His face was battered and bruised, had swollen badly on the left side. He stared from face to face, as though he dared someone to make a remark.

Roderick signaled with one hand to the sheriff. He grabbed Curly's shoulder, halting the tall cowhand. Judge Porter stopped, too. He seemed tired, and he stood motionless while Roderick talked.

"We won't need any papers," Roderick said to Nye. "Judge's got what he needs now."

"Bushwhacked?" Nye said, nodding toward upper Buffalo.

"Bushwhacked," said Roderick. "Thompson and Wayne are back there. Tobrez was right, Jaff. The Mexicans weren't in on any of this. And Charlie had nothing to do with the smuggling."

Roderick looked at Judge Porter. The judge nodded slowly.

Jaff Nye jerked his shotgun at the jail. "Take him inside." He glanced at the mob, caught the mention of Chico and Haven in the low talk that was going on. "Break it up now," he said. "Go on home."

There was murmuring and movement, but the crowd was no longer hostile. He watched the men in front of him. The word had sifted through to the rear. They were stunned by what they'd heard. Their guilt in the lynching was a blow. It was taking time for them to absorb the shock.

Nye lowered the double-barreled gun, letting the muz-

zle point to the ground. He said nothing, just stood and
watched as the men on the walks and porches turned
away slowly and headed off in all directions.

Bainbridge handed Roderick the keys to the cell block.
"Jaff'll be in in a minute," he said. "You wanna wait?
I'll take Curly inside."

"No," Roderick told him. "I'll lock him up."

He unlocked the heavy iron door and Curly walked
along the corridor ahead of him. In the closest cell
Stewart, a shocked expression on his bearded face, sat up
noisily in his bunk. The hostler's body was pressed close
to the bars in the last cubicle.

At the fourth cell Roderick halted Curly. "Right here,"
he said. He inserted the key in the lock.

Harry Stewart said, "Curly, you let him take you?"

"You shut up," Curly said. "You done enough talkin'
by now."

"I didn't talk, Curly! Not one word. It was Ernie who
talked." Stewart added tensely, "You ask Roderick if I
talked?"

Not answering, Curly stepped into the cell, but the
sober, grudging glance he gave Stewart didn't hide the
annoyance in his bruised and swollen face. He sat on the
bunk. Slumped forward a bit, without his thonged-down
guns, he didn't look formidable. He was just another man,
very confused. The iron door clanged shut, its vibrations
echoing along the corridor. Behind Roderick, footsteps
sounded, and he glanced over his shoulder.

Coming toward him was Bainbridge, who jerked one
thumb back at the office. His face was serious.

"Lucy Porter just come in," he said. "Her aunt set you
up, huh?"

Roderick nodded. He pulled the key from the lock, held
it out to Bainbridge.

From the end cell the hostler said loudly, "You got
them all, you can let me out."

"Let you out?" Bainbridge said.

"You got them all." He grinned confidently. "I'm in
no danger now."

"Well," Bainbridge said, "the sheriff'll decide about
you." He nodded at Roderick. "Jaff wants to talk to you."

Roderick turned and left the cell block. In the office,

Nye was standing near the desk with Judge Porter and Lucy. They did not speak as Roderick crossed to the gun-rack and put the shotgun back into place.

Through the windows Roderick saw that only a few people were out in the street now, but if they were talking or making any noise, it did not carry into the small room. He looked toward the desk when Nye said, "What you want to do about Mrs. Porter?"

"What about her?" Roderick took two steps forward and stopped directly below the overhead lamp. He stood and waited.

"She set you up," Nye said. "You got a right to prefer charges."

Judge Porter said quickly, "She was trying to protect me, Sergeant. Don't blame her." His face had turned white, and his lips trembled.

"You prefer charges, I'll go get her," Nye said, feeling the harsh decisiveness of the moment. He knew Roderick was filled with anger, but he was calm, and into that calmness Nye reached for his answer with, "She's at Harsbro's. She won't run, Will."

"I'm to blame," Judge Porter said in a choking voice. "I'll stay here."

Roderick opened his lips, then closed them. His glance had switched to Lucy. She was watching her uncle. Roderick read the pity in her face, and the kindness and sympathy.

"There'll be no charges, Jaff," he said.

Nye nodded, but it took several moments for this to register with the judge. It did, finally, and his shoulders sagged.

"Thank God," he whispered.

Lucy looked at Roderick now. Something in her eyes held him, something he had hoped would be there.

"Thank you," the judge said to Roderick. "We'll make it up." He was sincere, but the words sounded trite.

"You go on home," Nye said quietly. "I'll see you to-morrow."

"But I knew about the smuggling," the judge said. "You'll want me."

"Tomorrow, Judge," Nye said. "You won't run."

Judge Porter stared at the sheriff, hesitating as though he wanted to say more. But then the old man turned and started for the door. Lucy followed behind him. Quickly,

Roderick went onto the boardwalk. Lucy was just going past the window. He called her name.

She looked back and stopped. He walked to her.

"I'll be here for two more weeks," he said. "Tomorrow I'll come out to your house."

Lucy shook her head and looked at her uncle. "They'll need time. They'll need my help."

He nodded.

She smiled and took his hand and held it against her cheek. "We'll have our own time," she said. Then she continued along the walk.

Roderick stood watching her until a movement in the doorway broke the quiet. He looked back and saw Sheriff Nye standing just inside the threshold.

Nye pointed to the bloody bandage on his neck.

"You should have Doc look at that," he said.

Nodding, Roderick started to leave. But he stopped at Nye's question.

"You'll own that block that was burned down, once Chico's will is settled?" the short lawman said.

"The judge had some offers for that, Jaff." And, seeing Nye's thoughtful expression, "Why?"

"Don't sell for a while. That was the main place the Mexicans had for their own. Hold it till I can figure somethin' out."

"You want to buy it, Jaff?"

"No." Nye was staring towards Mexican Town. Roderick looked that way. Center was deserted down there. Only three or four lights showed from the shacks. In the moonlight the stovepipes stood out at crazy angles over the odd-shaped roofs.

Nye said, "This town's got a long way to come back. I can figure somethin' out."

Roderick nodded. "I won't sell," he said. "Take as long as you want, Jaff."

Nye nodded. He didn't speak as Roderick stepped across the boardwalk and down to the street.

Nye watched until Roderick had crossed Center and was almost to Doc Merrill's house. Then he went to the desk and opened a bottom drawer. He took out a hammer and went to the door of the cell block.

He said to Bainbridge, "Will you stay here till I git back?"

"Okay, Jaff." Bainbridge came into the office.

Sheriff Nye went outside.

A minute later a quick banging sounded in the direction of the hardware store in the adjoining block. Bainbridge went quickly to the doorway and looked out. A screeching of nails being pulled from wood sounded loudly.

"You okay, Jaff?" Bainbridge called.

"Yeah . . . yeah. You get back inside," Nye answered. He rested the "No Mex" sign he held against his knee and pounded the protruding nails flat. Then he tucked the sign under one arm and continued on to the next building.